What can you expect in Harlequin Presents?

Passionate relationships

Revenge and redemption

Emotional intensity

Seduction

Escapist, glamorous settings from around the world

New stories every month

The most handsome and successful heroes

Scores of internationally bestselling writers

Find all this in our November books—on sale now!

MISTRESS TO A MILLIONAIRE

*She's his in the bedroom,
but he can't buy her love...*

Showered with diamonds, draped in exquisite
lingerie, whisked around the world
in the lap of luxury...

The ultimate fantasy becomes a reality.

Live the dream with more
MISTRESS TO A MILLIONAIRE titles
by your favorite authors.

Available only in Harlequin Presents®

Maggie Cox

THE MEDITERRANEAN MILLIONAIRE'S MISTRESS

MISTRESS
TO A
MILLIONAIRE

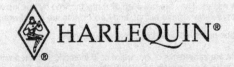

TORONTO • NEW YORK • LONDON
AMSTERDAM • PARIS • SYDNEY • HAMBURG
STOCKHOLM • ATHENS • TOKYO • MILAN • MADRID
PRAGUE • WARSAW • BUDAPEST • AUCKLAND

ISBN-13: 978-0-373-12584-5
ISBN-10:   0-373-12584-4

THE MEDITERRANEAN MILLIONAIRE'S MISTRESS

First North American Publication 2006.

Copyright © 2006 by Maggie Cox.

www.eHarlequin.com

Printed in U.S.A.

All about the author...
Maggie Cox

MAGGIE COX loved to write almost as soon as she learned to read. Her favorite occupation was daydreaming and making up stories in her head; this particular pastime has stayed with her through all the years of growing up, starting work, marrying and raising a family. No matter what was going on in her life, whether joy, happiness, struggle or disappointment, she'd go to bed each night and lose herself in her imagination.

For many years she secretly filled exercise books and then her word processor with her writing, never showing anyone what she wrote. It wasn't until she met her second husband, the love of her life, that she was persuaded to start sharing those stories with a publisher. Maggie settled on Harlequin as she has loved reading romance novels since she was a teenager. After several rejections, the letters that were sent back from the publisher started to become more and more positive and encouraging, and in July 2002 she sold her first book.

The fact that she is being published is truly a dream come true; however, each book she writes is still a journey in "courage and hope" and a quest to learn and grow and be "the best writer she can." Her advice to aspiring authors is "Don't give up at the first hurdle, or even the second, third or fourth, but keep on keeping on until your dream is realized. Because if you are truly passionate about writing and learning the craft, as Paulo Coelho states in his book *The Alchemist*, 'the Universe will conspire to help you' make it a reality."

CHAPTER ONE

SHE'D lost her best friend and discovered she wasn't who she thought she was—all in the space of a few weeks.

Two unrelated but cataclysmic events which had cat-apulted Ianthe from safety into the frightening sphere of the unknown, and in the painful process introduced her to a whole other reality.

'Well,' she said. 'Now that I'm here, I may as well make the best of it.'

Frowning in the mirror at the doubt she saw reflected so clearly in the rich caramel depths of her dark brown eyes, she tried to stem the tilting sensation that made her feel as though she was desperately endeavouring to keep her balance when a deep fissure had just cracked open beneath her feet.

'Keep breathing…just keep breathing.'

Her own advice rang a little hollow round the plain whitewashed walls of the hotel room, with its lone faded picture of a Greek Madonna and child—but still she grabbed at it, standing perfectly still until some of the terror ebbed away and she was breathing normally again. A slow trickle of sweat meandered down the valley between her breasts. She would fight this...she *had* to. There weren't any safety nets any more to catch her if she fell.

From the moment she'd decided to fly out to the small Greek island she had chosen at random on the map, with a tumultuous mix of grief and excitement pounding through her heart because that was where she would start her quest of self-discovery, Ianthe had promised herself that she would avoid anything that remotely resembled routine. She would discover an adventurous spirit inside herself if she had to take a shotgun to it and force it out.

'There's no going back, Ianthe, so you may as well get used to the idea and just accept it.'

This time her advice didn't ring so hollow, and a strong surge of determination made her feel as if she was being carried along on a jetstream of renewed purpose. She was twenty-nine years old, until recently the owner of a thriving and successful business, and would not argue the fact that so far her life had been fairly unremarkable. The beloved only child of parents who had already been in their forties when she was born, she had been brought up with caution instilled into her very marrow, so that she almost never did anything spontaneously, and Ianthe hadn't ever rebelled against that.

Until three months ago, that was—when the tumultuous events that had overtaken her had propelled her into acting in a way she had never acted before.

Locking the door of her room, she hurried down the wide 'Roman baths'-style steps that led to the hotel's small reception, suddenly needing to be amongst people again. Her flip-flop sandals slapped almost too loudly against the cool marble as she walked, so that she was conscious of the echoes being the only blemish on the otherwise subdued atmosphere. Depositing her key in the appropriate box on the wall, she went outside into a blaze of sunshine and a cornucopia of scents. She didn't really have a clue what she was going to do with her first full day on the island, but after all wasn't that the point? Instead of planning practically every moment to the nth degree, she would let the day take her wherever it willed. She would open herself up to opportunity instead of trying to predict every outcome.

As she set off down the shiny, slippery-stoned alleyway, Ianthe silently ordered herself to relax her shoulders and slow her stride. She was on holiday, for goodness' sake, not running a marathon! She breathed in with another passionate burst of determination, inhaling air that was crammed with the scent of so many delicious things it was hard to pick out just one. All she knew was that the balmy cocktail was stimulatingly different from anything she'd experienced in a long, long time.

Minutes later, sitting outside a waterside taverna that

had royal blue cloths on the tables and matching umbrellas, Ianthe focused interestedly on the outrageously glamorous yachts that were moored in the harbour in front of her. They seemed to positively yell *Look at me!,* their luxurious clean lines and gleaming bodywork fascinating her, yet eliciting little envy. Even unimaginable wealth was not armour enough to protect a person from the crucifying agony of being betrayed or losing someone you loved.

Ianthe had lost her best friend Polly to breast cancer when she hadn't even known how seriously ill she was. Less than three months later, when she'd been undergoing a routine blood test and the technician had innocently enquired what nationality her parents were, a seed of doubt about her ancestry had lodged itself in her mind and would not go away. There had been a couple of other occasions in the past when that same doubt had surfaced, and she had tentatively questioned her English-looking parents and been firmly reassured. In retrospect, she knew that she had never been quite convinced, but she had accepted their word and pushed the niggling questions determinedly away.

But this time she hadn't banished it to the back of her mind. This time she had confronted her parents with her nagging suspicion, demanded the truth, and had had her doubts shockingly proven correct.

Be careful of what you look for because you might just find it. That had turned out to be an adage Ianthe wished she had taken heed of, because she had learned that her parents were not her real parents at all. When the full, almost unbelievable story had emerged, she'd discovered that she'd been adopted as a baby after being abandoned by her natural mother in a hospital laundry basket, with nothing but a creased little note that simply read, *Her name is Ianthe.*

Now, as she raised her creamy almond latte to her lips, she blinked back the scalding surge of tears that swam into her eyes behind her huge black sunglasses. But she was unable to halt the flow entirely. No, money couldn't protect you from the events of life that hit you unawares, slamming you out of safety into a dark, dark chasm with no bottom on which to plant your feet. That was why Ianthe had put her business up for sale—the two fashionable dress shops that had cornered an eager market in boho chic and retro—and decided to ditch her predictable and safe routine for ever.

Now she was free of ties of any kind, and her life was an unknown trail that led to heaven only knew where. She would have to take comfort in the unknown from now on, because she had no job to return to, no romantic partner to worry about where her little quest of self-discovery would lead her, and no best friend in whom to confide. As for her parents... Well, she'd had the first really big row with them of her life. Why had they left it until now to tell her that she was adopted? Would they have told her at all if she hadn't confronted them with her suspicions? Why had they *lied* to her, deliberately keeping from her the astounding revelation that she'd had a brother too, who had died when he was only four years old—a year before they'd adopted Ianthe? That was why they'd been so over-protective of her—but part of the way they had 'protected' her was by lying.

Even Polly had lied. She'd lied to Ianthe to protect her, Polly's husband Tom had told her afterwards, because she'd known that news of her prognosis would devastate her closest friend. Her parents' defence of their own lies had been frighteningly similar: she would have been devastated. It had left Ianthe wondering why they all thought she was so incapable of dealing with the truth.

A deep shiver of distress rippling down her back, she took another sip of coffee, only to find it had cooled disagreeably and wasn't nearly as delicious as she'd promised herself it would be. Paying her bill, she left some coins for the waiter as a tip, pushed herself to her feet and made her way to an art gallery that was mentioned in one of the island's brochures she'd picked up. Her plan was to lose herself in there for an hour or two, and hopefully find some inspiration about what on earth she was going to do next with this precariously unpredictable new life she'd suddenly and perhaps recklessly signed up for.

Lysander Rosakis climbed out of the small fishing boat with ease, gave a brief salute to the man who had accompanied him but who was going on to a restaurant in another cove to sell his catch, laughed when his companion of the morning called out a witty reply, then headed back along the road beside the harbour to his house. As the sun beat down in a steady throb of heat onto his already sun-drenched limbs, Lysander tried to push away the little nugget of unease that arose in the pit of his stomach. He couldn't name or account for his fear right then, but he didn't have to. He was already well acquainted with what it was.

The last time he had stayed in the plain whitewashed house on the island he had been with Marianna—his wife. Now he was visiting the holiday destination he so loved alone. They'd come out to the island two summers ago now—just a couple of months before their baby was due—trying desperately to put a plaster on the gaping wounds of the previous year, when Marianna had had an affair. Lysander recalled that summer with pain, his footsteps slowing a little as the bittersweet memory cruelly submerged him. How could he have known then that his misery at the brittleness of his marriage would be devastatingly compounded by the dreadful events that had occurred on their way home to Athens? That Marianna would give birth to their son prematurely and, shockingly, that neither of them would survive?

A slashing hot pain knifed itself deep into his temple, and he drew his hand there in an automatic attempt to make its throbbing cease. But the acute discomfort was distressingly obstinate and, coupled with his frustration and rage at God for not intervening in the terrible chain of events that had blighted his life, it meant Lysander could not withhold the ripe curse that emanated from his lips.

What had he done to deserve such living torment? Hadn't he been a good Greek son? Following his illustrious father into the shipping business, forging his own equally illustrious career path, becoming a force to be reckoned with and revered amongst his peers? Hadn't he shelved his own compelling desire to make photography his career in lieu of carrying on the family tradition? Marianna had never understood Lysander's photographic work. She had sided with his father, loving the kudos and social cachet that marriage to a man of his wealth and lucrative associations had brought her, which even her own family's distant but much-mentioned connection to the aristocracy was not able to provide, and had constantly urged him to put aside his 'crazy' dreams and concentrate instead on being a successful businessman. Now the fruits of his success had definitely palled, and Lysander hardly knew what to believe in any more.

Marianna's betrayal, and then her death along with his expected child, had created scar tissue deep within his soul that would probably never really heal. The whole experience of marriage had left him with a scathing regard for romantic relationships that almost reached the point of contempt. His youthful dreams of a loving family of his own had crashed and burned, and changed his life undoubtedly for the worse. He might at last be making strides with his consuming passion— photography—these days, as well as continuing as head of the Rosakis business, but he was more alone than he'd ever been in his life. He had no son and no wife, and had developed an increasing preference to keep himself to himself—apart from occasionally seeking the company of a few close and trusted friends.

Thankfully, this was one of the few places he could come to in Greece where he would be largely left alone. The local people knew of the tragedy he had suffered, of course—the gossip grapevine extended to most of the outlying Greek islands, and with the illustrious name of his family, how could it not? But the islanders were respectful and kind, even protective of his privacy, and Lysander was grateful for that.

Almost wishing he had gone on to the other cove with his friend, instead of returning home to an empty house to eat lunch alone, he glanced towards the high walls of his friend Ari's art gallery. The twin doors to the cool interior were flung wide open in the almost midday sun and, making a spontaneous decision, Lysander decided to go in.

The brutally frank black and white portrait of on elderly Greek woman fascinated Ianthe. The personal suffering that all but poured from the sorrowful dark eyes that gazed back at her, swathed by a myriad of deeply etched wrinkles, no doubt hard earned, had called out to Ianthe the moment she'd walked into the gallery. As she'd crossed the cool wooden floor of the large ground-level room, its pleasant inviting ambience created by the subtle lingering plume of cedarwood incense that hung in the air and the painted saffron-coloured walls, Ianthe had all but had to keep herself from running towards the amazing study of the woman. She'd visited every other room to study the photographs on display, but she kept coming back to this particular work again.

It was no less than compelling. A stark illustration of a life pitted against tragedy and pain and probably hard physical grind that would test even the strongest, most determined being—and all beneath a cruel, unforgiving sun that, twinned with poverty and endured every day, could no doubt bleed the soul dry. The face was a triumph of survival over disaster—of holding on when even the thought of living through another sun-scorched and battle-scarred day seemed almost too much to bear—and it touched something deep and grieving that begged to be released inside Ianthe. She didn't know how she knew so much about an unknown woman, but she did. The power of the portrait was such that it revealed everything.

Her emotions raw, Ianthe found herself empathising with the woman's unspoken agony. The study touched the dark places inside her where rage, betrayal, a helpless sense of abandonment and a deep fear about her parents preferring the son they'd lost to their adopted daughter reigned supreme these days.

So absorbed was she by the portrait that at first she didn't notice the tall, straight-legged man dressed in jeans and a black T-shirt who had come to stand just a couple of feet away from her to share the perusal of it. But something about his presence seemed silently to command her and, unable to resist, she helplessly glanced sideways to see who had disturbed her.

Ianthe was caught up in a shocking vortex of vivid sensation as her eyes collided with the stranger's. She felt as if she'd been pierced by a hot velvet arrow that had gone straight to the very centre of her and, with devastating eroticism, had started to make her melt. He had tousled honey-blond hair cut in a deceptively casual style, a strong, arrogant jaw enviably chiseled—the kind you almost never saw in the street—and the most startlingly vivid blue eyes she'd ever encountered, the colour of a rain-washed summer sky. What were they? Indigo? Violet? Whatever the name of the hue, they were pretty amazing. And they had made her legs go weak as a marionette's.

Acutely aware that she was doing something she almost never did, and that was to gawk, Ianthe started to turn guiltily away.

'*Ya sas*,' he said smoothly, his voice a deeply resonant velvet question mark that made everything inside Ianthe tighten almost beyond bearing.

'Hi,' she responded, frowning faintly. She hadn't been expecting him to acknowledge her, let alone speak to her, and she was shocked that he had. Deliberately diverting her gaze back to the photograph, she told herself to wait for just a couple more seconds before politely walking away to look at something else.

'You are not Greek?' he commented in perfect English, a brief and speculative smile touching his smooth, sculpted lips. Her glance helplessly gravitated to the taut sinewy bulge of his bronzed biceps. They looked so tight the sight of them made her mouth water, and Ianthe fought hard to get control of her frankly dazzled reaction.

'Um...no. English. I'm English.' Shrugging apologetically, she started to back away from the photograph that had so enthralled her.

'You could be Greek.' He shrugged too, and totally floored Ianthe with the look of frank examination he casually bestowed on her face and figure. 'I expect you get told that all the time—at least in Greece?'

It was true. In almost every shop she'd looked into yesterday evening after her arrival, and before she'd had her dinner at a local taverna, she had been greeted in a flood of Greek by people expecting her to understand and respond. It had added shocking credence to the conclusion the police had made at the time of her discovery as a baby in the hospital laundry basket twenty-nine years ago. On the note that her real mother had left tucked inside her clothing the word *'Ianthe'* had been written both in English and Greek. Therefore, it was highly likely that her natural mother had been a Greek national—possibly working in London in a nearby hotel as a chambermaid or some similar occupation at the time of her daughter's birth.

'People look at my hair colour and eyes and I suppose they assume…' Not another word would come out. Unease and unexpected melancholy suddenly gripped her, and Ianthe made another move to leave her riveting companion to enjoy his examination of the mesmerising photograph alone. She was completely unprepared when he seemed to want to pursue their conversation.

'You like this picture?' he asked, meeting her gaze.

Diving into an intoxicating sea of blazing blue, she found that her purchase on readily available words was in worryingly short supply. Was she really expected to look into eyes like that and come up with a coherent sentence?

'I like it very much.'

She hated the way she sounded so nervous, as if she'd never even spoken to an attractive man before. Licking her moisture-deprived lips, she endeavoured to explain her feelings about the photograph. 'But I almost feel like I'm intruding on some great sorrow when I look at it, to be honest. It makes me want to give her some comfort. I would love to know more about her—the woman in the picture. The photographer must be a genius to have captured so much, don't you think?'

'He is a long way from being a genius, I can assure you.'

'You know him?'

'This is my picture.'

'You mean...you own it?'

'I mean I took the photograph.'

His expression unsmiling, he turned and examined the canvas with what appeared to Ianthe to be a more critical than admiring eye. Stunned that on her first visit to the gallery she should meet the creator of the most compelling piece of work displayed in it, Ianthe knew that her pleasure and her astonishment must show equally on her face.

'Well, you must be very proud of your work. I think it's wonderful,' she told him unreservedly.

His interest undeniably provoked, Lysander studied the woman in front of him with more curiosity than he cared to admit. She was not stunningly beautiful, as Marianna had been, but she was very, very pretty, with big dark eyes and a lush pink mouth. As he'd approached the woman in front of his photographic portrait—coincidentally his personal favourite of all the studies he had taken—after admiring the long dark hair that reached halfway down her back and gleamed with the sheen of a black pearl, Lysander had of course noticed that she had a very arresting figure too.

Her white linen trousers emphasised a perfectly edible peach-shaped bottom, gently flaring hips, and a waist that might easily be spanned by a man's hands. When he'd finally seen her from the front he'd observed with frankly male pleasure that she was nicely endowed where it mattered. In her pink sleeveless silk top, she had a sultry, womanly shape that any red-blooded male would more than appreciate. He liked her voice too. There was something quite engaging about her flat English vowels that intrigued him.

All of a sudden, Lysander knew that he did not want her to go and leave him alone. For once he was tired of his own morose company, and needed a pretty diversion like this enchanting young woman in front of him.

'I thank you for your compliment.' He smiled.

The young Greek woman supervising the entrance to the gallery just then inserted a new CD into the player on the desk in front of her. As hypnotically beautiful harp strings and a Celtic voice started to fill the air, Ianthe's attention was momentarily stolen from her surprised companion.

'Oh, what is this? It's lovely!' she enthused, her dark eyes shining. And Lysander's resolve to not let her run away from him became virtually a mission. The pretty English tourist was clearly someone who appreciated the beautiful things in life, and it would be pleasant to while away a couple of hours in her company.

'We will ask my friend Leonie to tell us what it is on the way out,' he replied confidently. 'I would like to take you to lunch. Would you do me the honour of joining me?'

'I don't think I—'

'You are here with your husband or boyfriend, perhaps?'

'Neither.' Ianthe felt hot colour flood into her cheeks. 'I'm unattached...at present.'

Why, oh, why had she told him such a thing? Now maybe he'd think she was expecting something more than just a lunch date!

But he seemed pleased with her answer all the same.

'Well, my name is Lysander, and if you check with Leonie in a moment or two she will confirm to you that I am indeed the photographer who took this portrait, and well known to both her and her husband Ari. There. I have told you my name, and now you must tell me yours.'

'Lysander?' Ianthe frowned, thinking. 'Wasn't he something to do with the Spartans?'

Her comment was so surprising that Lysander laughed out loud with pleasure. At the front desk, Leonie glanced over in surprise, and smiled at the sight of Lysander Rosakis apparently enjoying the company of an attractive woman again.

'He was a Spartan general. Not very popular with the Athenians, since he defeated them to end the Peloponnesian War. How did you know that?'

'I'm just interested in history.'

She went very pink as she said this, and Lysander studied her even more closely. 'It is a fascinating subject,

I agree, but I am still waiting to hear your name,' he reminded her.

Did she want to have lunch with this handsome stranger? He intrigued her for sure, but how did she know that she could *trust* him? Ianthe fretted. She was alone on this island, with no one to even know or care if something happened to her…

Oh, don't be so ridiculous! Her own voice came back at her in irritation. *Nothing's going to happen to you other than that you might just have a good time. For goodness' sake, Ianthe, live a little!* That last was Polly's voice. How many times had her wonderful and often ex-asperated friend urged her to do just that? Especially when Ianthe had been prevaricating over some invite or social event, making pointless heavy weather of some-thing that should be pleasurable. Sometimes her parents' endless pleas for caution became a ponderous chain, shackling her.

She made up her mind. Remembering what she'd promised herself, about taking every opportunity that came her way now that she was miles away from the known and the familiar, she found herself giving the ter-rifyingly attractive man beside her a determinedly agreeable smile.

'My name is Ianthe.'

He hadn't furnished her with his surname so she took her lead from him. After lunch she would probably never see him again, so it hardly mattered. Somehow it would be fun to stay anonymous…to be a different Ianthe, not bound by her usual self-imposed restrictions and conformity.

'But you have a Greek name!' His eyes narrowing as he continued to study her, Lysander did not conceal his surprise.

'Yes.' She shrugged almost guiltily, unable to explain that she was on a bit of a personal quest—that she might truly be able to claim some Greek blood, except she didn't know how or even if she would ever find out the truth about her own ancestry.

'Come.' He moved beside her and lightly touched her hand—not missing the look of startled pleasure in her unbelievably sultry dark eyes. 'Let us go to lunch together and we will talk some more.'

CHAPTER TWO

'So, HOW do you go about choosing subjects for your pictures?' Ianthe asked him before biting into an olive she'd selected from her colourful bowl of traditional Greek salad. They were sitting outside at a taverna up on a hill, the sparkling iridescence of the sea a stunning backdrop as two passenger ferries crossed each other in the distance, leaving a foaming backwash in their wake.

Lysander appeared thoughtful for a moment, his captivating eyes shielded from her gaze by dark sunglasses. Even so, Ianthe felt the keen scrutiny of his unsettling glance with the same stunning acknowledgement as though he was asking the most intimate questions of her that a man could ask a woman…

'The woman in the photograph became my subject quite by chance,' he replied with a shrug, breaking some bread and leaving it on his plate.

Her glance was drawn immediately to his lean, bronzed hands with their almost pearlescent square-cut nails. He definitely had 'artistic' hands, but they didn't look work-shy either.

'I'd been travelling around some of the smaller islands, taking my camera with me, and after walking all day in one particular place, and getting lost, I stopped at a small house to ask the way. It was Iphigenia's house—the woman in the picture. She fed me that day with what little food she had, and in the course of our meal together she told me her life story. When we had finished eating she was curious about my camera and asked if I would like to take her picture. I said of course, and the result you see in the gallery.'

Iphigenia had moved Lysander deeply that day, with her kindness and her humility. Their encounter had happened just three scant months after Marianna had died. Leaving his business affairs to trusted colleagues, he had taken off travelling, needing to be alone for a while, needing to make sense of a world that he could not pretend to understand any more. Iphigenia had lost her entire family to illness, one after the other—her husband, her son, then lastly her daughter. Yet she wasn't bitter, and she was utterly convinced that they would all be reunited again when she died.

Lysander had almost made his own entreaty to God that that might become true for her, though he nurtured no such similar hope of being reunited with the baby son he'd lost. That would be a miracle he found too hard to believe in…especially when he knew he probably didn't deserve it. He had never been able to shake a nagging feeling that maybe, because he hadn't truly been able to find forgiveness in his heart for Marianna's adultery, he was somehow being punished.

When he'd finally returned home and developed the picture he'd known he'd captured something very special indeed. He could have sold Iphigenia's picture a hundred times over with the interest it had generated, but Lysander had instead given it to his friend Ari Tsoukalas to hang in his gallery.

'So you are a photographer by profession?'

'Amongst other things, yes.'

There was not the slightest need or inclination on Lysander's part to tell this charming young woman that he earned his main income from the shipping industry, and that that income ran into millions of dollars a year. Far better that she believed him to be a simple photographer. That would allow them both to be free to enjoy their unexpected lunch together, without all the baggage that his family's name and wealth entailed.

'And do you exhibit your photographs anywhere else?' Ianthe enquired politely. For a moment Lysander's attention was caught by the way she chewed on the juicy black olive and carefully extracted the stove by making her mouth into an unconsciously sexy 'O' shape, to capture it with her forefinger and thumb. Such an ordinary, commonplace action should not provide the highly provocative entertainment it did, but Lysander couldn't deny that his groin had tightened hotly at the sight. He considered the pretty English tourist with a renewed fascination that wouldn't be assuaged.

'Not yet, but I'm currently working on putting a small exhibition together in Athens with a friend.'

He was telling the truth—apart from the fact that the exhibition was being held in one of the city's most prestigious venues, and the friend who was helping him put it together was one of the world's most celebrated photographers. It wasn't anything to do with any kind of social nepotism, though: Lysander's photographs had caught the other man's professional eye when some of them had been published in a fashion magazine.

'Well, I wish you well with it. If your other photographs are anything like the one I saw today then I'm sure you're well on the way to making your fortune.'

She smiled, showing perfectly neat straight white teeth. Lysander didn't doubt that she dutifully brushed them and flossed three times a day. Already he'd sensed that she was a contained little thing, the kind of person who paid rigorous attention to the small things in life… yet he'd also intuited that underneath she had a fire in her belly to match his own. A person who could be spontaneously moved and inspired, as he'd seen her that morning, would not lack for passion.

As the hot sun beat down upon their heads, Lysander fell into a compellingly erotic little daydream about how he'd like to spend the rest of the afternoon igniting

that passion he was so certain she possessed into full unfettered flame, and the realisation of what he was contemplating did not induce the remotest sense of guilt.

He wasn't looking for a soul mate. Emotionally, he
was spent: there was nothing left in that department to
give any woman. These days Lysander had only one use
for attractive females who persisted in trying to
command his attention. Ianthe might not have deliberately come on to him like the others usually did, especially when they found out who he was, but she had
confessed to him that she was unattached. It wasn't
beyond the bounds of possibility that a woman like her
would be nursing some secret hope of some kind of
romantic liaison whilst on vacation.

Well, he couldn't offer her romance. But the idea of
a liaison—now, that was appealing.

'Thank you. But I have done all the talking, it seems,
and I still know nothing about you. What brings you to
our little island?'

She didn't answer him straight away. It was a rela-
tively simple question, but she seemed to be having extraordinary difficulty finding a reply.

'I came because I badly needed a break…a change
of scenery.'

'And you travelled here alone?'

'I didn't want to travel with anyone because I needed
time on my own, to think.'

'That sounds very serious. So you have important decisions to make about your life, perhaps? Or am I being a little too personal?'

He *was* being too personal, but when he removed his stylish sunglasses and fixed her with that arresting indigo stare of his Ianthe did not have the nerve or the inclination to rebuff his questions. In any case, 'too personal' or not, it might be easier to share some of what was on her mind with a stranger—someone she would never see again once she left the island.

Ianthe decided to take at least a small step and reveal something of what she felt—just not too much.

'I suppose I do have some important decisions to make. Some things…some very hard things happened that have kind of forced those decisions on me. But the truth is, in some ways it's as though what happened—how it affected me—was fated. Up until recently I was ignorant of personal tragedy or pain. I think I needed to learn that lesson, however painful, and change my way of life.'

She went quiet for a very long moment. Lysander could see the near agony that she could not quite conceal in her very expressive dark eyes and was curious at what had caused it.

Then she took a breath and smiled, deliberately lightening the mood. 'Of course it's far easier to contemplate than actually do, don't you think? Making changes, I mean.'

'If the desire is there…' He shrugged. 'I think you have clearly been changed already by what has happened to you, Ianthe. You are a brave woman to embrace it so philosophically. Many people recognise they need to change something, but rarely do anything about it—even when pushed. It is too easy to pretend nothing has happened, or stay in our comfort zones, no?'

He was so easy to talk to. His deep, rich, accented tones seemed to lull her into a strange feeling of safety she hadn't experienced with anyone else. And he'd said she was brave. No one had ever said that to her before.

She closed her lips and became very aware of the silent but strong clamour of emotion surging through her heart.

'Ianthe?' Lysander prompted gently, his hand reaching for hers.

Contact with his firm, warm flesh was like being seared with a branding iron, and for a moment she was caught up in a vortex of shock and heat that robbed her of speech.

'I'm not brave at all,' she insisted after a while, her shock slowly subsiding as she stared down at her small slender hand, held possessively captive in his. 'I've been the opposite all my life. Always playing safe, always erring on the side of caution. My parents tried to protect me from everything, you see, and I'm afraid I just let them.'

'But now you are breaking free, yes? Like a beautiful butterfly emerging from a chrysalis.'

His words caused such a swell of emotion inside her that Ianthe pulled her hand free and rubbed it, biting down on her softly quivering lip to prevent herself from disgracing herself with tears. She had to change the subject to something less personal. 'This is such a beautiful place…have you always lived here?'

She was determined to bring their conversation back to much more neutral and safe ground. When Lysander didn't immediately reply, but instead surveyed her as though he understood every raw emotion that was threatening to submerge her—and understood it intimately, as though he was a kindred spirit—Ianthe found she couldn't look away from him, no matter how hard she tried.

'I don't live here. I only visit now and then. I have a house on the island, and whenever I need to get away for a while…this is where I come. I live in Athens. And, yes, I agree with you, this *is* a beautiful place. It is a good place to come when you have lots of thinking about life to do.' His voice was gently humorous, but not in any way derisive.

'Is that why you're here too?' she asked him, feeling as though she stood precariously on the edge of a precipice that hypnotically begged her to leap into space. She took a hasty sip of the chilled white wine he had ordered for them with their meal, but her hand was trembling as her fingers curled round the stem of the glass.

Surprisingly his jaw clenched a little, as if her question disturbed him.

'No. I am here on a kind of working vacation.'

'Taking photographs, you mean?'

'Ianthe?'

'Yes?'

Startled by the suddenly authoritative tone in his voice, she felt her brown eyes collide anxiously with his searing gaze, like the fragile wings of a moth bumping against the dangerous yet compelling heat of a lightbulb.

'As flattering as it is to have a woman so easily persuade me to talk about myself, I am much more interested in learning about *you* than in answering all your very polite questions about my own life.'

He was being perfectly serious. Especially since holding her hand just now had engulfed him in the kind of heat that stirred the blood to passion rather than friendship. Just an hour or so ago he had been feeling angry and in despair—hating his own morose company, but still unable to contemplate spending time with anyone else. And yet now…now, after being with the sweet, sexy woman sitting opposite him for just a few short minutes, he felt more vitality throbbing through his veins than he had experienced in months.

'I don't really want to talk about myself, if you don't mind,' she replied. 'I'd just like to sit here and enjoy the sunshine and your company, and forget about my problems for a while. Is that all right with you?'

Apart from taking her to bed and tangling his limbs with hers for the rest of the afternoon in the trapped heat of his bedroom, with the blinds rolled down to shield them from the unforgiving sun, Lysander couldn't think of anything he'd like better.

'You don't ask for much. And I would be happy to

sit here and do just that.' He raised his glass to her in the semblance of a toast. 'I am very fortunate to have met you today, Ianthe. I thought it would be a day just like any other, but meeting you has proved me wrong, I do believe.'

Feeling her face radiate a heat to match that of the sun's rays, Ianthe met his warm, searching glance with mixed feelings of pleasure and alarm fizzing inside her like lemonade bubbles. Turning her head away, she deliberately focused on the sublime scenery instead—silently and fervently calling upon divine help to prevent her from dangerously succumbing to the myriad and infinitely fascinating qualities of this wildly attractive and unusual man.

Lysander had been unable to resist inviting Ianthe to join him for dinner. He'd refused to consider the question of whether it was wise of him or not, and now he could barely contain his great desire to see her again as he sat at one of the best tables on the terrace of an exquisitely positioned restaurant overlooking a presently calm ocean, the sun almost ready to demand homage as it set.

He spied Ianthe at the entrance, talking to an animated young waiter, and his chest tightened oddly at the sight of her. Even though she stood several tables away from him, he could sense the hum of admiring interest that her appearance was generating. He experienced a small, yet almost violent reflex low down in his belly—part jealousy, part pride that for tonight at least she was his—and with every moment that passed he realised he was growing more and more impatient for her to join him.

She was wearing a simple red and white halter-necked cotton dress that paid loving homage to breast, hip and thigh before flaring slightly and falling elegantly to just below her knees. With her rich dark hair as shiny as a sunlit river flowing prettily down her slim back she was stunning, and observing her in those arresting few moments gave Lysander a picture that he would not soon forget. Sensual excitement dealt him another stunning blow.

He stood up as she arrived at their table, the young waiter deferentially arranging the chair opposite his for her to sit, and flushing ever so slightly beneath his perfect olive skin. Lysander guessed that perhaps the young man was embarrassed at being noticed talking so animatedly to the wealthy Lysander Rosakis's new ladyfriend.

Thanking him in his native tongue for showing his guest to his table, Lysander waited until his charming dinner companion sat down before addressing her.

'I am very glad that you could make it,' he asserted, his gaze locking possessively onto her shy brown eyes.

'Am I late?' she anxiously returned, glancing down at her watch in dismay. 'It was such a perfectly lovely evening that I couldn't resist just strolling.'

'I arrived early, so, no, you are not late. You are just in time to witness one of the most spectacular sunsets, in fact.'

They both glanced towards the blazing orb hovering just above the sea's edge, sending a ricochet of intense orange flame scudding across the already darkening waters. Ianthe sucked in her breath.

Hearing the unbelievably sensual little sound, Lysander felt the smile on his lips melt abruptly away— so taken aback was he by her innocent yet at the same time passionate response to witnessing one of nature's most awe-inspiring wonders.

'Doesn't that stir your soul?' she demanded, her eyes wide, briefly moving her glance back to Lysander's.

Marianna had never noticed a sunset in her life. He doubted it would ever have occurred to her to consider whether she had a soul, let alone ask him about his. Ianthe's words struck an answering chord inside him, deeply and provocatively.

'Yes, it does,' he replied, his voice low and slightly husky. 'No matter how many times I am privileged to witness it, its beauty and power never fail to move me.'

He had the most amazing voice, Ianthe thought as a flare of heat exploded inside her breast. Hearing it was like bathing in a warm bath scented with her favourite perfume. In fact, it was one of the most delicious sensory experiences she'd ever had…perfect for seduction.

The all too tempting idea escaped her characteristic self-restraint like wild horses chasing a dream, and for a while Ianthe succumbed to it with undeniable relish. But cold reality quickly surfaced. She hadn't agreed to have dinner with Lysander in the hope that he might seduce her. She'd heard all about the pitfalls of holiday romances even if she'd personally never experienced one, and a man as dynamically attractive and charismatic as him had probably had his share and regarded them as fleeting pleasures that he would quickly forget. For all Ianthe knew, he might even be married.

This new thought filled her with horror. As charming and compelling as he was, she would no more consider having an affair with a married man than she would walk down her conservative suburban high street naked! That was one opportunity that she would definitely *not* be taking!

'What will you have to eat?' he asked, breaking into her thoughts afresh with that sensual, provocative cadence of his voice.

Taking the menu he offered, and glancing only briefly down at its lacquered pages, Ianthe cast her gaze almost immediately back to his.

'Please don't think me presumptuous, but…' How could she put an undeniably indelicate question delicately? His relaxed contemplation of her face did not waver at her words, but seemed to become more disturbingly concentrated. Little implosions of panic and awareness were like landmines dotted along her vertebrae. She swallowed. 'You asked me if I had a husband or a boyfriend. Well…do you mind if I ask you the same quest—?'

'My wife died.'

His voice was as bleak and foreboding as a deep, dark well—the kind that she would not dare to look down in case there was something menacing and dangerous lurking in there. He did not bother to hide his complete distaste for her nervously executed question. The hue of his disturbing eyes suddenly resembled impervious blue marble, and it appeared as if the Lysander that Ianthe had sensed herself succumbing to with such surprising vehemence had suddenly vanished—in his place was a cold, forbidding stranger. A horrible shiver licked slowly down her spine.

'Now that that is clear, and you know that I am not trying to involve you in some kind of illicit love affair, perhaps you would care to think about what you would like to eat, Ianthe?'

Her throat dried so hard that she gazed longingly at the carafe of water on the table between them, almost willing it to levitate and come to her rescue.

'I didn't mean to offend you in any way, Lysander.'

A disconcerting dimple appeared at the side of his tanned cheek and confused her altogether. 'Of course you did not. Now the matter is at an end. Forget about it and we can concentrate on enjoying our evening together.'

Ianthe wanted desperately to know what had happened to his wife. How had she died and how long ago? It was clear he must have loved her deeply, going by the jagged rip of pain she had momentarily glimpsed in his eyes before that distinctly frosty barrier had slammed into place to guard against unwelcome speculation.

It was clear, Ianthe thought, that those areas were taboo: topics that she didn't dare raise again unless she wanted to incur his deep disapproval and maybe even wrath.

Forcing herself to scan the menu again, she was taken aback when he softly pronounced her name.

'I did not mean to upset you.'

'I'm not upset.'

Shaking off her uneasiness with a forced smile, Ianthe found herself unable to glance away as quickly as she'd intended, so that she wouldn't expose her sudden unhappiness. It wouldn't have worked in any case. Lysander's reaction was like quicksilver.

'Do not lie to me, Ianthe. You are the kind of girl who wears her heart in her eyes, and I am not blind.'

CHAPTER THREE

WHEN he'd seen his father's favourite yacht, *Evangeline*, moored as regally as a queen in the picturesque harbour, amongst other well-known cruisers belonging to the wealthy Athenians who inhabited the tight-knit monied world of the Rosakis family, Lysander's heart had truly sunk.

It could not be mere coincidence that his father had decided to visit the island at the same time that his only son was taking a break there. Therefore, Leonidas Rosakis had to want something of him. Last year he had almost lost his life when he'd contracted pneumonia, but mercifully he had rallied, and ever since that time he'd seemed to be on a mission to control his only son's destiny even more. His main concern, of course, was the future of the shipping business that had made his family's fortune, and his brush with death had heightened that concern to an almost obsessive degree.

Now, as Lysander boarded the wide steps leading to

the main deck, a white-shirted member of the yacht's crew dipping his head deferentially as he passed him, he found his thoughts racing ahead to Ianthe.

Last night after dinner, when he had walked her back to the small hotel where she was staying, he had but grazed her cheek with his lips as a kiss goodnight. But both he and she had registered the intensely electrical reaction that their contact had ignited, as though their bodies had been plugged into a generator. Ianthe had looked startled and wide-eyed as he'd drawn away, and Lysander had had to hold his burning desire in painful check all the way home, the memory of her warm skin beneath his lips arousing his senses into almost a crescendo of powerful need.

What did she possess that held him in such extraordinary sensual thrall? When he had first met his wife he had found her astonishing beauty alluring, but he could not honestly recall almost wanting to crawl out of his skin with the need to possess her…as he did with Ianthe.

She had agreed to meet him in about half an hour's time at the harbour, where Lysander had arranged for one of the locals to take them to an outlying private cove to picnic and sunbathe. Nikos was discreet and would not repeat any conversation he might overhear to anyone else… Lysander would not have hired him otherwise.

Now, as he forced himself to think about why his father's yacht should be here in the harbour, he made his way hurriedly past the formal dining room into the main salon, where he guessed he would find the man in question. Unable to deny his impatience to bring their coming encounter to an abrupt and swift end, all Lysander wanted to do was return to the waterside taverna where he had suggested Ianthe wait for him.

Leonidas Rosakis lived up to the leonine connotations of his name. There was no doubt about that. An inch over six feet tall, he was still a formidable-looking man, even though he had recently been cut down by illness. He was the proud owner of an enviable head of abundant silver hair, and had a presence that could easily impinge authority and awe on the very air around him. Yet at the same time he was not so much lion as pussycat with his two young grandchildren, the offspring of Lysander's sister Evadne, and could be as tender as he liked when he chose.

Right now, as Lysander approached the huge oak desk that practically took up one complete wall of the stately salon, his father threw him a glance that was anything but tender. Old resentments deeply held surfaced, and he had to swallow hard to clear the tension already building inside his throat.

'What are you doing here, Father? I only saw you in Athens a few days ago.'

'Such a cold greeting from my only son!' Leonidas intoned dramatically in his deep belljar of a voice. 'What have I done to deserve such disdain?'

Releasing an impatient sigh, Lysander tunnelled his

fingers restlessly through his hair, instinctively knowing that he had a royal battle on his hands when it came to controlling his temper around his father.

'I do not demonstrate disdain so much as irritation that you should show up here, when you know only too well that I needed to get away from Athens and be by myself for a while...*without* any interference from the family!'

'You call fatherly concern *interference*? Shame on you, Lysander! You should know me better than that.'

'I know you only too well, Father.... That is why I do not entirely trust your motives for being here. What is it you want of me? Are you unwell again? Do you want me to speak with your doctors?'

'First you break my heart with your caustic admission of distrust, then you enquire about my health!' Shaking his great leonine head, Leonidas sighed deeply, as if enduring a terrible wound. He walked round his desk so that he stood a scant foot away from his handsome, if somewhat suspicious-looking, son.

'Actually, I have some good news for you. Some very good news that I hope will put a more—shall we say *amenable* expression on that scowling face of yours!'

Immediately alert, Lysander swept his blue eyes over his father's now smiling visage with a sudden wave of presentiment flooding through his insides. 'Good news' was subjective when it came to Rosakis family dealings...especially where Leonidas, the undoubted patriarch, was concerned. It was only natural, going on past experience, that Lysander should view it with suspicion.

'What is this good news you have to tell me, then? Tell me quickly, so that I can be about my business and return to my vacation.'

The old man's smile wavered just a fraction on his indomitable face. Leonidas gave the distinct impression that he was choosing the words he was about to use particularly carefully—picking them like prize cherries out of a tree. He and his son did not always see eye to eye, but at that moment Leonidas was praying hard that his imminent announcement would fall on far more receptive ears than, unfortunately, he suspected they might.

'I saw an old friend I hadn't seen for years yesterday…' He paused, calculating the impression his words were making so far on Lysander, but his son's expression remained infuriatingly blank and unreadable. 'Takis Koumanidis. We went to school together. Remember—I told you about him?'

Lysander responded with a very brief, almost imperceptible flash of acknowledgement in his guarded blue eyes. 'Last year he took over…' He mentioned the well-known name of one of the most illustrious shipping lines—a name that Lysander realised immediately his father would love the opportunity to merge with at the very least. He instantly felt the tension across his back and shoulders grip harder—like a band of iron almost bending him in two. What was the old trickster up to now?

'That's right. Now, do you remember he had a daughter? Well, Electra is now twenty-two and, having met her at dinner last night with Takis, I can report to you that she is a girl of exceptional beauty and intellect. She has been educated at the best schools in Paris and Rome and has exquisite taste in almost everything. Takis was telling me how she longs to settle down and have a family, but sadly as yet she has not met the right man. I could not help but think that you would be perfect for her, Lysander. It has been over two years since your wife died...long enough for you to start thinking about marrying again. I would like you to come back to Athens on Saturday and meet her. When I told her all about you she was much interested. "Intrigued" was the word I believe she used...'

Clenching his jaw to try and contain the slow-burning rage that was gathering momentum inside him like an electrical storm about to wreak havoc, Lysander stared at his father with the bitterness of profound anger and dismay rising like bile inside his throat. Releasing a violent expletive out loud, he strode impatiently to the opposite end of the luxurious salon and back again in a bid to control his rapidly escalating temper.

His suspicions had been right. If only for once in his life where his father was concerned Lysander could have been proved wrong. If only Leonidas had just once demonstrated even the remotest understanding of what his only son had gone through, then the rift between them might have started to mend. But, as it was, Leonidas seemed to dismiss the hurtful events of Lysander's recent past with astonishing ease.

There had been no acknowledgement of the devastating emotional onslaught and grief he had endured. He had married, for his father's sake, a woman whose alluring looks and falsely loving demeanour had deceived him as to the true nature of her character, who had cruelly betrayed him not once, but twice. And then, just when they had been trying to rescue the jagged pieces from the inevitable wreckage of their declining relationship and Marianna had become pregnant, both she and their expected son had lost their lives.

If his father had expressed sympathy for all that, had ever apologised or even acknowledged his own part in making the disastrous marriage, then Lysander could have forgiven him almost anything. But his father's approach to his son's distress had been shockingly pragmatic and unemotional. And now here it was again. He should just put his appalling marriage, Marianna's death and the demise of his unborn child aside and go headlong into another arranged dynastic marriage so that he could have an heir.

Lysander was ready to explode at the fact that the old man was trying to inveigle him into a marriage of convenience with the daughter of a fellow shipping magnate.

He could see the old man's point, of course. It would be a merger that would not only unite two exceedingly powerful and wealthy families, but would turn their mutual assets into an even more formidable force to be reckoned with in the business world.

And never mind what the personal cost would be...

'You are unbelievable—do you know that? How dare you even raise the subject of my potential remarriage? You are well aware that I am still grieving for my lost child, as well as dealing with the aftermath of a marriage that destroyed my faith in that doubtful institution ever again! Let me be perfectly clear about this once and for all. I am not *remotely* interested in meeting the daughter of your so-called old friend, either socially or for any other reason, and neither am I interested in remarrying! I have been through the fires of hell, Father, and I would not wish the experience on my worst enemy. But all you can think about is the profit to be made!'

'Show some respect where it is due, Lysander, and do not speak to me as though I was the dirt beneath your feet! I only have your best interests at heart. I only *ever* have your best interests at heart. Do you think it pleases me to see you a mere shadow of the vital young man you were, not interested in either the business or the family? All right, so you may not be ready to enter into another marriage, but you could at least meet Takis's daughter, couldn't you? What would it hurt? You would have someone pretty to take out to dinner once in a while at least, instead of spending all your free time dabbling in that ridiculous hobby of yours!'

Reluctantly returning to the big leather chair behind his impressive desk, Leonidas lowered himself into it with apparent difficulty, a spasm of pain crossing his face as he finally seated himself. Lysander could not help the answering jolt of deep concern inside his own chest. But at the same time he was furious with his father for disparagingly referring to his photography as a 'ridiculous hobby'. The truth was, nothing was as important or compelling to Leonidas Rosakis as the family shipping business, and he simply could not fathom why Lysander should not feel the same.

'Are you all right? Shall I call someone?' he asked reluctantly, biting back the fresh wave of anger that engulfed him as he studied his father's distressed face.

Leonidas gestured him impatiently away. 'I am fine—if a little aggrieved by your hard-hearted attitude to my honest concern for your future welfare. Why can't you just come back to Athens on Saturday and have dinner with your mother and me?'

And Takis Koumanidis and his 'beautiful' and 'intrigued' daughter Electra, no doubt.

Lysander shook his head firmly. 'I'm on vacation and I have no desire to return to Athens until my vacation is at an end. You will just have to entertain your friends without me.'

'Very well, then. Go. But at least ring your mother

at the house and let her know you are all right, eh? All she ever does these days is fret about you, Lysander. And if you *should* get a little bored with snapping your pictures, then do me the honour of coming home for dinner on Saturday after all, yes? You can go straight back to the island afterwards, and I will leave you in peace for the rest of your vacation. I promise.'

'I have already given you my answer and I see no reason to change it. I'll be seeing you around, Father. Don't over-exert yourself. And you may tell Mother that I will ring her soon.'

Without another word, Lysander turned on his heel and swiftly left the salon, with its gleaming rosewood surfaces and antique furniture. He sprinted down the wide steps of the luxurious yacht back onto dry land, where he could hopefully breathe more easily again.

Ianthe had woken up that morning with a line of butter-flies doing the conga in her stomach. At first she hadn't known why...then she'd remembered. She was meeting Lysander at the harbour and they were sailing out to a charming little cove that he knew of where they could swim and talk in private.

Now, as she lay in bed covered with nothing but a thin cotton sheet, she pushed back her hair from her forehead as she nervously contemplated the day ahead. Staring up at the plain white ceiling, she couldn't help wishing for some kind of sign from up above that would signal to her that this was an opportunity she shouldn't miss, and not some wrong turn she should expressly avoid.

She was perfectly free to decide for herself either way, of course, but she was coming to realise that sometimes free will could make an already difficult choice even more difficult.

Exhaling softly in frustration, she raised her fingers to her cheek and wonderingly touched the spot where Lysander's lips had brushed against her skin so devastatingly last night. Closing her eyes, she sensed his kiss all over again, and a buzzing effect like the hum of electricity started at the tips of her toes and travelled all the way up to her scalp.

She didn't even know his full name—she barely knew anything about him—yet already Ianthe knew that Lysander was having the same inevitable effect on her as scorching sunshine had on a block of ice.

An hour later, as she nervously searched for him amongst the throng of holidaymakers already seated outside some of the several waterside tavernas that lined the route, the rest of the world seemed to disappear when she glimpsed his tall, straight figure strolling casually towards her. Her footsteps drew to a nervous standstill as she tried to calm the wild, fluttering sensation inside her.

He was so beautiful…a magnificent depiction of strong and sensual masculinity bar none. He had a way of walking that was authoritative and compelling even when apparently relaxed, and that forever after would help Ianthe pick him out from a crowd of thousands at just a glance. Yet underneath the undoubted confidence he exuded there was a surprising hint of vulnerability, and it was that thought that entrapped her curiosity and inexplicably pierced her heart. Even though she suspected that her intuition was probably wrong on that count, she still couldn't resist becoming intrigued by the idea.

She was wearing a dusky pink sundress with a deep neckline, and beneath the ivory-coloured straw hat that was fetchingly circled with a bright pink ribbon she'd fashioned her lovely dark hair into two loose plaits. The look was hardly the height of sophistication, but on Ianthe it was no less than perfect and engaging. Purest pleasure expanded like a sunburst inside Lysander's chest. The instant he saw her the unhappy exchange he'd just had with his father was swept straight from his mind, relegated to an unhappy mental filing cabinet where he already had a catalogue of difficult exchanges with his father stored away for future and probably bitter examination.

The sight of her pretty face reminded him of the exquisite perfection of a dewy pink rose, and it touched an unexpectedly fierce longing for his own lost innocence deep inside him. Lysander instantaneously needed to get Ianthe by herself, away from the busy harbourside that was already teeming with holidaymakers. His desire almost broke free of its bonds, making him want to do something completely spontaneous and rash—like kiss her in public.

He almost succumbed, but caution dictated that he did not, in case any too-interested observers might be watching. Already he knew he was taking a big risk that his father might hear of his liaison with a pretty English tourist, and right now Lysander wanted no more of his father's unwelcome interference in his life. Leonidas would be even more dismayed to hear about his son's new 'romantic' interest when he was so intent on getting him to meet the rich and beautiful Electra Koumanidis. But, for now, Lysander was determined that nobody would intrude on his desire to be with Ianthe—*nobody*.

'*Ya sas*,' he greeted her gravely, the hunger in his intensely blue eyes for the moment kept secret behind his sunglasses as they travelled at will across the alluring contours of her strikingly pretty face.

'Hello,' she said back to him, equally serious.

'Are you ready to go?'

'I think so.'

She glanced down at the striped straw bag swinging from her arm, which contained her towel, swimsuit, suncream, bottle of water and the latest novel she was reading. Not that she imagined she would feel inclined to read for one moment with the challenging distraction of a young Greek god lying next to her in the sun. But she'd included the book because she'd worried that he might at some point get bored with her conversation or company and just want to be by himself. How could she know how he would react when he was still an unknown entity to her?

The instant her thoughts travelled down that particularly unhelpful road, Ianthe's frustration with herself magnified. She'd been a successful businesswoman, for goodness' sake! She knew how to talk to people, how to make interesting conversation—so why was she selling herself so short? She couldn't keep blaming Polly's death and her parents' at times stifling over-protectiveness for such negative behaviour. She had to remember that she was the one in charge of herself, that she didn't have to succumb to the unhelpful conditioning of her past.

'Let's go, then.'

With an enigmatic little smile playing about his sensually sculpted lips, Lysander placed his hand authoritatively beneath Ianthe's elbow. She allowed him to steer her away from the crowds towards the other end of the harbour, where she assumed they were meeting the boat—and the further away they travelled from the other tourists, the more Ianthe sensed Lysander relax.

As she walked along beside him, only too aware of the excitement that had buzzed along her nerve-endings when he'd touched her, she glanced at the glamorous yachts floating serenely in the water and honestly didn't envy any of their owners in the slightest. They might possess wealth beyond her wildest dreams, but Ianthe had the day, and the added compliment of the gorgeous man walking next to her, wanting to spend it with her.

Her best friend had died, and she had found out that she wasn't her parents' natural child. But right at that moment Ianthe didn't wish for anything other than what she had.

CHAPTER FOUR

NIKOS moored the boat in a corner of the cove, roping it to a nearby wooden stake at the end of the purpose-built little jetty.

Ianthe received the distinct impression that not too many people knew about this private little haven, but it was clearly used by those in the know, or else the jetty wouldn't be there. Following Lysander out onto the pretty sweep of beach, that was literally a secluded cove hewn roughly out of the landscape, Ianthe was momentarily glad that Nikos had moored the boat and was staying with them for the duration of their stay there.

All of a sudden it hit her that she and Lysander were the only occupants of the beach, and for several long seconds her stomach churned with nerves at the reali-sation. In a way, she wished that he *hadn't* kissed her last night, because she couldn't get the memory of how it had felt out of her mind. She could swear that his lips had left a mystical brand on her cheek when they'd touched her skin, and even now it tingled fiercely as her recollection deepened. Such an innocuous little brush of flesh on flesh shouldn't cause the veritable seismic upheaval that she was still feeling, but—shockingly—it did.

She had been without a relationship for too long, that was the trouble. Why else would she feel as though she were walking on hot tarmac in bare feet around an attractive man like Lysander?

There was a little group of sunbeds arranged together on the sand. Laying down his rolled up towel on the ground and stripping off his shirt, Lysander pulled two apart and arranged them together a little way off from the others, underneath a large straw umbrella whose stem had been set into a small block of concrete to keep it steady. He did all this without speaking, and Ianthe watched the muscles in his bare torso ripple and stretch taut as he bent to move the loungers, her heart nearly stopping when he finally straightened and delivered a smile so sinfully provoking that her feet were rooted to the ground.

'Is this not a good position?' he asked, shaking out his towel and spreading it on one of the beds.

Clearing her throat with difficulty, Ianthe forced her frozen lips into what she fervently prayed was an equally relaxed smile, although she feared it looked more like an expression of terror.

'It's fine. It's very…secluded here,' she commented, pushing her sunglasses further up her nose as her gaze nervously scanned the beach.

'Give me your towel,' Lysander commanded, and when Ianthe had passed it over to him from out of her straw bag, he shook it over the sunbed, grinning with amusement as her stylish little black bikini spilled out first.

She'd meant to change into her swimsuit back at the hotel, and leave it on beneath her sundress, but she'd been so anxious, anticipating the boat trip with Lysander, that she'd automatically rolled it up in her towel—as she did at home when she went swimming. Now it struck her that she would have to change behind a handy rock or bush somewhere if she wanted to put it on for a swim, which didn't exactly help her feel particularly elegant.

A small bead of sweat rolled down her spine between her shoulderblades at the thought of undressing anywhere near this man.

'You will want to get changed somewhere,' he said to her, holding out the bikini so that she could retrieve it.

'I should have changed back at the hotel, but I...I must have got distracted,' she admitted, one shoulder lifting in an explanatory little shrug as she took it. 'I'm okay for now. Actually, I think I'll just lie here for a while and read my book, if you don't mind?'

In answer, Lysander's disturbing lips curved into an unsettlingly knowing little smile. Stripping off his shorts, he casually undressed down to his swimwear. Ianthe's startled gaze fell helplessly upon hard-muscled, toned limbs, feathered with fine dark blond hairs, and the skin underneath of tanned, shimmering bronze. She was instantly suffused in drowning heat at the sight of all that masculine physicality on display for her personal delectation.

'I am in definite need of a long swim,' he told her, jerking his head towards the deceptively calm aquamarine ocean lapping at the shoreline. 'So enjoy your book and I will see you in a while. If you need anything from the boat to eat or drink, just ask Nikos, okay? I've told him we will eat lunch around one.'

Barely able to tear his glance away from Ianthe's long slim legs, arrestingly showcased in the pink sundress as well as that tormenting glimpse of cleavage, Lysander came to the rapid conclusion that his body needed the shockingly icy contact of freezing cold water to cool it down—and needed it right now. Nikos had also noticed Ianthe's stunning figure on the boat—what man with breath in his body would not?—and had made a ribald joke to Lysander about it that had instantly provoked his anger. It frankly amazed him that he should be so jealous about other men ogling a woman he had only just met, on whom he had no claim on other than that of brief acquaintance.

Now, as he strode across the sand, he contemplated the fact that he could have taken Ianthe to a far more glamorous beach than this one. But then they would not have had the privacy or seclusion they had here. And, more importantly, there was no doubt that Lysander would have been forced to explain his wealthy background, because to use the beaches that he and his friends frequented you had to be a member of the club— that monied, élite little circle inhabited only by the fabulously rich. He didn't want to do that. His main goal for today was to simply just enjoy Ianthe's company— and if that manifested into an opportunity to entice her into bed, then Lysander would not be slow to take advantage of it. He was just discovering that now they were here together he did not feel at all inclined to share her delightful company with anyone else. Least of all inquisitive friends or colleagues who naturally would want to know who Ianthe was and, equally naturally, would no doubt report his attractive new companion to his father.

She'd fallen asleep beneath the shade of the straw umbrella with her book left open on her lap. But the hot sun had still brazenly visited her bare feet and calves, and now they prickled uncomfortably in the scorching heat as Ianthe opened her eyes and sat up in a daze.

She'd been dreaming about her mother. She hadn't been able to make out her features at all, but she'd had long dark hair, just like Ianthe's own, and she'd spoken to her as though she were a small child again, tenderly. So tenderly that Ianthe was hit by a sense of longing so profound that she was momentarily frozen in the poignant tragedy of her loss, her heart aching almost past endurance for the chance to know the woman who had given her birth.

Taking a long, shuddering breath, fiercely trying to blink away the hot tears that washed into her eyes, Ianthe was forced to give way to the feelings that kept pushing to the surface from deep inside her. Had her mother come from a place like this? Had she laughed and played with friends in a similar little cove to this one when she was growing up? Or had her daily life been all about the hard grind of physical work—trying to help make ends meet in a family like Iphigenia's, the woman whose sorrowful eyes had gazed back at her so heartrendingly in Lysander's revealing photograph?

Searching in her bag for the bottle of water she'd brought, because her suddenly achingly dry throat needed relieving, Ianthe tried to push away her unexpected distress. After taking a drink, she stared unseeingly out to sea.

What had caused her poor, desperate mother to travel to England and give birth to her baby in the kind of circumstances that had forced her to leave her child in a hospital laundry basket for someone else to take care of? Ianthe's parents had told her that the police had searched for her mother for a long time but with no luck. She had simply disappeared without trace. What upset Ianthe more than anything was that she must have needed medical help after giving birth. Had there been anybody to help her? And what had become of her lover, the man who had fathered Ianthe? What had happened to him?

Lost in her thoughts, she didn't register Lysander's arrival until he was practically beside her. If he registered the hurt that must have been plain to see on her face he gave no indication of it. Instead he glanced down at her bare legs and frowned, as though she were a child he'd given instructions to and he now saw with dismay that his instructions had not been obeyed.

'Come back to the boat,' he said tersely. 'You should get out of the heat for a while and have a drink.'

'You're burnt.'

With a disapproving shake of his dark blond head—damp as a seal's pelt from his swim—Lysander ran his fingers down one of Ianthe's bright pink calves, the unexpected touch making her flinch in surprising pain when it came into contact with her tender skin.

'I must have dozed off.'

'Did you apply some suncream before you fell asleep?'

Of course she had. She wasn't a total imbecile! 'I put plenty on—it's a high factor, too. The sun must have been particularly strong.'

Again Lysander glanced at her as though she didn't have the wits or wherewithal of an infant. 'Now you are going to suffer.'

So what was new? She seemed to have been doing nothing else lately.

Embarrassingly, tears swam into her eyes. Before she could wipe them away Lysander stilled her hand and cupped her chin. 'You need not suffer as much as all that, my sweet Ianthe. Sit down and I will apply some aftersun for you.'

'I—I should have gone for a swim with you.'

Lysander smiled unreservedly into her moist dark eyes. 'Yes, you should have. But never mind…there will be other opportunities.' Turning his head towards a clearly fascinated Nikos, he gave the other man some instructions in Greek and waited until the unshaven and laid-back skipper meandered obediently off the boat, lighting up a cigarette as he went.

'Where is he going?' Ianthe asked, feeling her shoulders tense.

A blaze of amused sky-blue almost dazzled her. 'He's going to take a walk. He spends a lot of time on this boat and he needs the exercise.'

'You're laughing at me.'

Feeling uncomfortably gauche, Ianthe knew her shoulders had stiffened even more. She'd never felt so acutely discomfited or affected by a man in her life, and it was making her act like a completely different person she didn't recognise.

'I would never laugh at you, Ianthe, believe me.'

Reaching for the aftersun, Lysander tipped a generous amount into the palm of his hand and, kneeling down before her where she sat on the padded bench seat, he started to gently smooth it onto her legs. She flinched again, but this time for a very different reason.

She found herself wishing that he'd put his shirt back on at least, if not his shorts. All that bronzed, toned and glistening flesh was too much for a girl to take in one fell swoop—let alone have him stroke aftersun onto her bare skin!

Touching her was making him hot—even though the reason he was touching her was not sexual at all.

While he'd taken his swim all Lysander had been able to think about as he'd ploughed through the water was the girl he'd left behind on the beach—too shy to even put on her costume to lie in the sun. The tragedy of his past, the strained relationship he had with his father, the near certainty that he was probably right about his scheming to hook him up with Electra Koumanidis and ruthlessly further the family empire— none of it had played for even an instant on his mind. It struck him forcefully with astonishment that a woman—even one who was such a surprising and delightful contrast with the beautiful and predatory sophisticates who so often came his way—had the power to enthral him so emphatically.

Just as Marianna had done when he'd first met her, after she'd been deliberately directed his way by his father. He shrugged off the thought impatiently.

This new attraction was both unexpected and undeniably appealing. He wanted to seduce Ianthe, yes…but would it be wise for him to go just that little bit further and get to know her? It would certainly not be in keeping with the way that he viewed attractive women.

Now, as he continued to stroke aftersun onto her slim calves—long after he'd fulfilled the reason for doing so—he glanced up to find her serious brown eyes assessing him with a mixture of bewilderment and longing reflected in their mesmerising depths.

He stopped still, his warm palms curled round the backs of her legs, his thumbs resting lightly on the skin at the front. The gentle sound of water lapping against the side of the boat became a meditative mantra that made him subconsciously listen out for each connecting wave. It created a kind of expectant tension in him. He heard Ianthe drag in a shuddering little breath and let it out again. The mingled scents of aftersun, polish, diesel and engine oil, trapped and baked by the sun, swirled around him in a soporific drift that seemed to render all his senses almost painfully acute.

Sensing the heat in him intensify, he slowly eased himself up onto his feet, catching Ianthe's hands as he did so. With a deeply rasping sound of uncontained need he dragged her hard against his chest, anchoring his hand behind her head and laying ruthless claim to her softly parted lips for the very first time.

Driven by nothing less than raw instinct and desire, the lust in him a maelstrom of power sweeping him passionately up into its centre, he plunged his tongue in deep, letting her sweetly moist flavours wash over him, setting up a sensual thrum in his blood so spellbinding that he almost surrendered his balance. And she did not resist, but provocatively matched him kiss for greedy kiss, her slender long-fingered hands locking onto his ribcage as if she too needed anchoring. She pressed herself even closer to him, the lush rounded curves of her breasts contained in her bra almost flattened against the steely muscles of his chest.

If they had truly been here alone Lysander would have had no compunction in taking the steamy passion they were generating to its ultimate conclusion. And judging by her mutually hungry responses, Ianthe would not have thought of refusing him. His tormenting, voracious need for her made him feel as though some delirium-inducing fever had taken hold of him. He simply *had* to have her! If he could lose himself in the seductive call of her warm and willing body, then for that blissfully sweet time out of time he could perhaps suspend past tragedy and the ponderous weight of family responsibility and experience a little of the light instead of the dark. How compelling was that thought?

But they were not alone. And Lysander had no intention of furnishing Nikos with the kind of scene that even he—loyal employee that he was—might perhaps be compelled to share a description of with his wife after

Ianthe and Lysander had left the boat…no matter how much he trusted the skipper.

Of course if he'd taken her out on one of his *own* vessels—that would have been a different story. But Lysander wasn't ready to yield his true identity to Ianthe just yet, and alter the dynamics of their still fledgling attachment. Not when he was enjoying the anonymity and relative freedom of being just an ordinary photographer in her eyes…

Ianthe sensed straight away the moment when Lysander started to withdraw from her. His kisses slowed, then ceased, and his warm breath feathered over her aching mouth like a tempting but regretful footnote. As much as she told herself he was clearly being the sensible one out of the two of them—that it was purely *crazy* to think that they could make love out here on the boat in broad daylight, with the very real possibility of the unshaven skipper possibly wandering in on them—she couldn't help longing for their passionate union. Lysander's sinful mouth, along with his strong hands and powerful body, had made her ache and throb and melt so forcefully that she was almost tempted to beg him to finish what they'd started.

Frustration bit down heavily on her already heightened nerves, like a steel wall clanging down in front of the gateway to an enchanting pasture, barring her entry. But she had to take a leaf out of Lysander's book and be sensible too. She'd come here on a quest of self-discovery—perhaps to search for clues to the woman who had given her birth and vestiges of the ancestry that ran through her blood—not to yield to a hot but doubtless brief little affair with some unknown local.

Stepping out of his embrace, because his hands had grown slack on her arms, Ianthe raised her hand to her hair to tidy it, her gaze shying self-consciously away from Lysander's even though she wanted nothing better than to gaze into his dazzling glance for all eternity.

'Ianthe?'

'Yes?' Her brown eyes collided apprehensively with stunning blue and she found herself repeating a fierce little mantra in her head while she waited for him to continue. *Don't tell me you regret what happened... don't say it was a mistake...*

'I want very much to make love to you, but Nikos's boat is not the place to give way to such desires. You understand?'

Ianthe let out her breath slowly and the mantra in her head subsided. She found herself floating on a dizzying ocean of pleasure that bathed her in blessed and thankful relief.

'Of course... I know that. Whew.' She smiled tremulously at him. 'It's so hot today, isn't it?' She wiped her hand round the back of her neck. 'I wonder what the temperature is outside?'

Lysander didn't know about outside, but in here the temperature must have already exceeded boiling point.

He could not help it. His hungry gaze dropped lasciviously to the enticing neckline of Ianthe's fresh cotton dress that revealed a teasing glimpse of lacy white bra and softly rounded flesh, so tempting and touchable that his loins flooded with heat all over again. His mouth dried and his skin tightened almost past endurance at the thought of dispensing with the virginal white bra that so inflamed him and feasting his lips on her no doubt tightly puckered nipples. Already Lysander had experienced a very provocative sample of what her pretty flesh tasted like, and all it had done was set up a near obsessive desire in him for more.

He reached a swift conclusion. At the end of the evening he would not be giving Ianthe any chaste or restrained kisses goodnight. He would be unequivocally suggesting that she return to his house and share his bed. And if anybody saw them together and reported back to his father, then so be it. It was none of Leonidas's damned business *who* his son slept with! It had not been in the past and it certainly would not be now. Lysander was *not* going to yield to any kind of pressure from him to court women like Electra Koumanidis for the sake of expanding their already billionaire status and increasing the Rosakis family business's power base. And he was *not* going to pass up the opportunity to take Ianthe to his bed.

'Let me go and find Nikos.' He addressed Ianthe, smiling. 'I think it is about time he prepared our lunch, don't you?'

CHAPTER FIVE

THEY had arranged to have dinner at one of the less busy tavernas, away from the inevitable hub round the harbour. It was situated down a pretty side street with vibrant red and pink bougainvillea climbing the whitewashed walls—not far from Ianthe's hotel. But now, as she sat outside waiting for Lysander to arrive, at a table covered in a bright red and white chequered cloth, the fragrant Mediterranean air a sweetly whispered caress against her already sun-kissed skin, she couldn't help but question the wisdom of agreeing to another date with him.

Today, out on the boat, she'd experienced one of the most powerfully erotic encounters she'd ever had. She'd been ready to give Lysander everything, she hotly recalled, a guilty stain of crimson creeping into her face. In one blisteringly sexy surge of desire she'd almost forgotten her own name, the day of the week, even what country she was in—never mind why she was here.

She was definitely courting heartbreak if she continued to see him. She was under no illusion that it would be easy when the time came to break off her attachment to him…and that time undoubtedly would come. She wasn't the kind of woman who could put something like that down to experience and simply move on. That knowledge had been slowly seeping into her consciousness all day.

That was doubly the case now, while her heart was still heavy with grieving for Polly. She was vulnerable emotionally—another good reason for avoiding emotional entanglement with Lysander. Ianthe was devastated that she couldn't write or phone her closest friend and share her doubts and fears.

And on top of that she was searching for some kind of connection…anything that might give her a clue as to who the woman who had borne her had been. In truth, she thought, she was looking for herself as well, because the true Ianthe Dane didn't exist—not really. How could she, when her whole life had been based on lies and deception? Her parents might have started out with the honest intention of protecting her from hurt— what child would want to know she was abandoned at birth?—but she'd been an adult for a long time. How could telling lies, suppressing the truth about her past, protect her from anything? Ianthe could scarcely understand how the two people she loved best in the whole world could have done that.

Feeling the weight of sorrow press heavily upon her

chest, like a wall that had tumbled down on her brick by painful brick, she reached for a glass of water and gulped some down. The waiter—quite a striking young man, whose brooding presence she had noticed—briefly inclined his head in acknowledgement towards Ianthe as he stood, arms akimbo, in the taverna doorway. He had vibrant, searching eyes and a lean body whose suppressed tension said he was waiting for his chance to escape the narrow confines of his family and his home. All that scarcely contained restlessness made Ianthe aware of his discontent, and she wished she could convey to him how lucky he was. She wanted to tell him not to be in such a hurry to escape something that one day he might long for. He was so fortunate to have such firm roots, an ancestry that was probably ancient, whereas she…

She couldn't do this. She was distressed, off balance, raw. To find out all the things she yearned to learn about the land of her mother's birth she had to be on her own, without any major distractions—such as an unforeseen love affair.

She tried to console herself with the fact that a dynamic, urbane man like Lysander would not be too upset at her breaking off their brief acquaintance. The good-looking photographer would soon find another pretty tourist ready and willing to enjoy a few hot Mediterranean days and nights with him, if that was what he was looking for…and Ianthe didn't doubt it was.

A wave of jealousy and regret rolled through her at the thought of him being with somebody else—of having those skilful hands of his touch someone else's body and not hers. Determinedly pushing the upsetting feelings aside, she rose to her feet, folded her jacket across her arm, unhooked the soft suede strap of her bag from the corner of her chair and prepared to leave the restaurant.

The young waiter whose palpable longing to be anywhere other than his home she had intuited came immediately over to her, not hiding his bewilderment.

'You are leaving without staying for dinner?'

'I—I have a headache. If my…friend comes looking for me, would you please tell him that I've gone back to the hotel to rest? His name is Lysander.'

'Okay, I will tell him. Perhaps you will come back tomorrow?'

'Maybe'

'*Andeeo*…goodbye'

'Goodbye.'

Shrugging lightly, anxious to be away before Lysander arrived so that she wouldn't have to make her explanations in public, Ianthe left the taverna and hurried away down the street.

Loud knocking on her door stirred her into full consciousness. She'd been lying on her bed fully dressed and must have momentarily dozed off. The room was too hot and stuffy, and she'd been seduced into sleep by enervating tiredness. Now Ianthe stared at the closed door for what must have been a full thirty seconds before calling out, 'Who is it?' Her voice was still shaky from the aftermath of sleep and sounded like a husky stranger's.

Even before her visitor replied she knew it was Lysander.

She should have waited and spoken to him face to face instead of running off like that. What had she been thinking of? The trouble was, she'd allowed her fears to dominate again, and had simply let them overwhelm her. She hadn't really thought her actions through, and now she regretted acting so impulsively.

'It's Lysander. Open the door, Ianthe. I want to talk to you.'

She could have pleaded a worsening headache, and the thought did cross her mind. But she wasn't a coward, and she would face him as she should have done in the first place. Anyway, he deserved an explanation—especially when he'd been kind enough to take her to dinner *and* hire a boat to take them out for the day.

'Wait a minute, then.'

She planted her feet on the floor by the side of the small double bed with its plain white cover and responded with a little shiver of pleasure to the luxurious sensation of cool marble against her soles. The temperature in the room was almost oppressively close. It hardly surprised her, considering that the distinctly old-fashioned unit that was meant to provide air-conditioning looked just about ready to give up the ghost.

'Why did you not wait for me at the taverna? Did you really have a headache?'

A brief, accusing flare of vibrant blue and he had bypassed her startled gaze and strode angrily into the room. Curling her bottom lip anxiously beneath her teeth, Ianthe slowly pushed the door closed behind them, urgently trying to strengthen her resolve against his almost overwhelming attraction.

The powerful disappointment Lysander had experienced when he'd arrived at the taverna only to be told that his 'lady friend' had gone back to the hotel with a 'headache' was not something he was willing to experience again soon. Nor had he welcomed the frankly suspicious look in the eyes of the waiter who had broken the news to him. It had clearly said, *What did you do to upset her?*

Lysander had guessed straight away that Ianthe did *not* have a headache. Instinct had told him that she had simply changed her mind about seeing him. The very idea had infuriated him—stabbed at his bruised ego like a pair of sharpened scissors. He might not have been actively seeking a relationship, but it was practically unheard-of for a woman to turn him down and he could not help but resent it. Since he'd been in his late teens Lysander had been used to having his pick of beautiful women. He did not deserve to have the first woman he had become fascinated with in the two interminable years since his wife's death reject him.

'I'm sorry it's so hot in here, but I don't think the air-conditioning is working properly.'

Her smile a little nervous, Ianthe slowly wiped her hand across her forehead. Lysander tracked the unconsciously sexy movement with a surge of volcanic heat inside him that focused his attention almost exquisitely painfully. Her simple gesture had riveted his gaze to the tempting upswell of her firm round breast in the pretty, diaphanous little peach dress she wore, and he had never experienced arousal so savage and spontaneous in all of his life.

'I'm sorry I didn't wait for you at the restaurant—that was rude of me. I wouldn't normally behave like that. But...the truth is, I feel like I've got involved in something that maybe I shouldn't have, and I didn't know quite what to do about it.' She frowned. 'You have to understand, I came here to try and sort out my life—not make it more complicated. As well as needing a holiday, there are—other reasons I've come here. If I was with you I wouldn't be paying proper attention to those reasons, and I *need* to. I think I should just be on my own for a while, to be perfectly honest. It's been lovely spending time with you, but all things considered, I think—'

She anxiously broke off mid-sentence, aware that Lysander was staring at her. His glance was both examining and bold. The sight of him made her suck in a deeply nervous breath and desperately try to curtail the flood of sensual heat that helplessly saturated her senses like decadent golden honey oozing through her bloodstream. The elegant white shirt and dark trousers he wore, coupled with the tan that lent such vibrancy and warmth to his skin, looked just too good on his arresting physique. His features were strong and chiselled and his dark blond hair defiantly tousled in deference to the overall image of smartness and respectability he exuded this evening—as opposed to the casual jeans and T-shirt he'd been wearing when they'd first met. In that garb he'd made a merciless enough attack on her slumbering libido, causing her to feel more acutely aware of long-buried needs than she'd ever felt before, but dressed as he was right now Ianthe didn't have a prayer.

Her stomach muscles almost screamed in pain with the effort of clenching them as she asked herself. Did she *know* what she was turning down? Did she even have an idea?

She watched him nod to himself, as if to absorb what she had just told him and digest it. Then he smiled. He was definitely not playing fair…

'Firstly, I think you are right about the air-conditioning,' he drawled, in a voice pitched disturbingly low. 'I will speak to the manager on out way out and get it fixed. Secondly, it is not such a good idea to be alone when you clearly have things on your mind that are troubling you. Sometimes it helps to talk. I think that you should come back with me to my house tonight. It will be much more comfortable than this far too warm hotel room, and I think that any conversation we must have about the two of us would be better accomplished there rather than here. Yes?'

Ianthe was categorically certain that the laconic 'yes' tacked on to the end of his sentence was merely a perfunctory adjunct that hardly required a response—because the tacit meaning implicit in his speech was that she definitely *would* be going back with him to his house tonight. No argument about that.

His indisputable arrogance pushed a very hot button for Ianthe. It reminded her of her father's almost dictatorial attitude towards her when he was convinced that he and only he knew what was best for her. Such as keeping her birth and parentage a secret! Well, she had decided that from now on she would be making her own decisions about her life, without interference from anyone else—and she simply was not going to allow this man to take charge, no matter how hard his attraction might be to resist.

'No, Lysander. I don't think that's a good idea. I think *I'm* the one who knows what's best for me under the circumstances. I'm sorry if my decision upsets you. And as for the air-conditioning, please don't trouble yourself about it. I'm quite capable of speaking to the hotel manager myself about getting it sorted out.'

He wished she would trust him with what was troubling her. Not that he could fix her problems, but he could not deny that he felt concern for her anxiety all the same. But right now, greater than his concern for her troubles was the fact that she was rejecting him.

Lysander had hardly expected Ianthe to turn him down a second time, but when he gazed back directly into her pretty brown eyes she appeared to be quite resolute. Her unexpected stance, not bending at all to his suggestion that she spend the night at his house, to take to its rightful conclusion what they had started out there on Nikos's boat earlier today, at the same time both infuriated him and inflamed his growing desire.

Out on the boat she had all but been ready to surrender her body to him completely. He wasn't delusional—he knew a willing woman when he held one in his arms. Now he couldn't help wondering if Ianthe knew who he really was, if she knew the cachet that his family's name carried with it in these islands, would she be as resolute in turning him down?

In less than a heartbeat Lysander's feelings had switched from a willingness to remain anonymous and carry on the pretence that he was just a simple photographer to a sudden yearning to wield the full impressive power and authority he had at his fingertips by virtue of his name—if that was what it took to get Ianthe to go to bed with him. He could hardly believe the crazy way he was thinking! But this woman, this self-contained

English girl, had stoked his desire almost to fever-pitch, and now he simply could not contemplate *not* having his lust for her reciprocated.

But, no. He wouldn't yield to his baser nature. Partly because he wanted Ianthe to like him for himself and not his wealth, and partly because he didn't really want to find out if money would be a temptation for her. He knew his disappointment in her would be colossal if he found out that it was.

He shrugged instead. 'You do not accept help easily, I can see that. You think that seeing me will complicate your life, but I think it could help you to feel better, Ianthe…even for a little while. Perhaps tomorrow, when you have slept on your decision not to see me again, you might wake up and think differently. For my part, I will sincerely hope that that is the case. If you need to get hold of me in the meantime, here is the address of my house on the island.'

He was writing on the back of a matchbook he'd pulled from his jacket pocket and he handed it to Ianthe with a faint frown creasing his brows. 'I know sorrow, if it is sorrow that you feel, Ianthe. Whatever secrets you have that are causing you pain, I can promise you that they would be safe with me. I will see myself out.'

Ianthe was still dwelling on his words, a mixture of surprise and emotion keeping her rooted to the spot, as he quietly opened the door and left her.

* * *

An old woman walked by the café where Ianthe was having her morning coffee. She wore a faded print dress and a black headscarf, and her weathered skin looked as shiny and brown as a cobnut. On her bronzed arm swung a basket, and as she passed the fruit and vegetable stand that was situated opposite to the café she ran her fingers through some fresh parsley then passed them under her nose to sniff the pungent scent that must have lingered there. The almost sensually elegant little action was like a perfectly choreographed ballet, and throughout the compelling little vignette the woman kept on walking, a 'Mona Lisa' smile playing at the corners of her lips, her hips swaying as she negotiated the slight incline of the cobbled thoroughfare in her worn-down shoes.

Watching, enthralled, Ianthe experienced a wave of yearning so intense that she almost wished she could have stopped the woman and talked to her. Would her own grandmother have been something like this woman? Would she have walked down a street such as this, just going on with the day, with a smile on her face, content with her lot and not asking for anything more other than that her children be safe and that there be enough money to put food in the cupboards? Ianthe instinctively as well as logically surmised that her mother must have come from a fairly poor family. Why else would she have been in England, working as a chambermaid or a waitress, perhaps, as her parents and the police had supposed? Why else would she have given up her newborn baby?

I know sorrow, if it is sorrow that you feel.

Lysander's words came back to haunt her, and suddenly her longing to know more about her mother and her background swelled into a different kind of longing entirely. This profound, bone-deep ache came from way down in the depths of her soul and was for a man with the most incandescent blue eyes she'd ever seen—a man who took photographs so powerfully beautiful that they could move the viewer to tears.

He laid down his camera to stare intently at the laughing young people diving off the harbour walls to swim in the sparkling ocean. Usually there wasn't a day or an hour, even a minute sometimes, when he couldn't find solace or pleasure in taking pictures. But today...*today* Lysander could take no comfort or pleasure in anything very much—including his photography. He had not been able to get Ianthe out of his mind. As well as desiring her almost beyond bearing, and craving her company, he could not get the untenable, almost unbelievable fact that she had *rejected* him out of his mind. Now all he could think about was how to win her back. Why did people always want the things they could not have?

Irritable beyond belief, he forked his fingers through his already dishevelled hair. Anyone looking in on his very privileged and fortunate life from the outside would no doubt think that Lysander had everything a man could want. What they did not see or know was that he missed holding someone close at night—someone who cared whether he lived or died. He actually hated sleeping alone. He missed having a lover, not just some pretty passing ship in the night, but someone he could spend a little time with, whose company would not quickly begin to pall…someone like Ianthe. For all his wealth and impressive connections, money could not buy him the things he craved the most.

In a despicably weak moment, during an impassioned telephone call from his mother that morning, Lysander had reluctantly agreed to return to Athens on Saturday night and humour his father by joining him at dinner with their guests Takis Koumanidis and his daughter Electra. His mother had told him that Leonidas had done nothing but mope around since he had last spoken to his son and she feared that he was making himself ill.

Seriously doubting that that was the case, and knowing that the old trickster was just sulking like a child because he had been unable to get his own way for once, Lysander had nonetheless capitulated to his mother's request. He adored Galatea, and it was not her fault that her husband liked to manipulate his family like pawns on a chessboard. Feeling even more irritable that he had to face the prospect of a dinner party he emphatically did not want to attend, and making small talk with his father's 'old friend' and his daughter—knowing that everyone would be watching him and Electra together and smiling encouragingly at every bit of trivial conversation they might be forced to make together—he picked up his camera from where he'd left it on a nearby rock and strode back down the hillside in a mood that was definitely bordering on black.

CHAPTER SIX

SHE'D have liked to say she'd hesitated about going to Lysander's house, but that would have been a lie. Ianthe was quickly discovering that there were some things in life you simply couldn't fight. One was the personal longing to grow, to stretch beyond your self-imposed limitations, however much it might drag you kicking and screaming out of your comfort zone. Another was your heart's desire, which had an amazing capacity to overrule the logic of the head.

The need to see Lysander again had consumed her to an almost feverish degree, robbing her of an even halfway decent night's sleep and filling her mind with nothing but him, as if he were the only thought that existed in the entire world. Now she was forced to ac-knowledge that she couldn't stay away as she'd planned. Cold, logical, sensible intention couldn't help her when her whole body throbbed with want and need every time she thought of him. Her helpless fascination for this man kept propelling her towards him instead of allowing her to keep her distance.

Now, gazing at the simple wooden landing that jutted out from the serene-looking whitewashed house that hugged the harbour, Ianthe clenched and unclenched her moist palms as fear and trepidation drenched her like a violent summer shower. Wiping them down the sides of her green linen shift dress, she almost prayed that Lysander wasn't at home, so that she could talk herself out of presenting herself to him like this. But even as the thought drifted by, barely explored, the sky-blue front door eased open and he stood there, shirtless and golden, eyes piercing her like flawless indigo laser beams, gazing at her with the same hunger and simmering, shocking need that pulsated like a lava flow through Ianthe's own veins.

'*Kalimera*, Ianthe. You have had breakfast?' he asked casually, as if he'd almost been expecting her to show up at his door this morning.

Mouth as dry as an Indian summer, Ianthe's shocked lips formed a tremulous answer. 'No.'

His hand enfolded hers possessively as his glance, irresistible and knowing, magnetised her. Then, with surprising gentleness, he drew her into the sensually filled coolness of the shaded room behind the door.

'So…you have not eaten breakfast and neither have I. What shall we do to feed our hunger this morning, hmm?'

'Lysander…' Her dark eyes pleaded for his understanding. 'I shouldn't have come, but I—'

'I missed not having you in my bed last night. Such pictures my mind conjured up of you, Ianthe, that I was in a fever of longing. Now that I see you here in the flesh that fever has grown worse. See?'

To Ianthe's alarm and consternation, Lysander placed her hand against his forehead and held it there for the longest moment. Then he smiled lazily, no doubt knowing full well that he held her in thrall, and brought her hand back down again to his side.

'I am burning up for you, and I think there is only one remedy for my condition.'

His fingers brushed the skin just behind her ear. Ianthe almost jumped through the roof. Until that moment she'd had no idea that that place was a veritable carnal touch-paper, or that it could engender such an explosion of lust at the briefest contact from this man's fingers. She could actually feel herself shake with need.

'Lysander… I—I thought about what you said, and—'

'I need no other explanation other than that you are here. I prayed that you would change your mind, and it seems that my prayers have been answered.'

'But we can't just—don't you think we should discuss things first?'

The words trembled on her lips, but she knew they were just a flimsy and not very effective attempt to delay an event that was as unstoppable as a raging river flowing downstream. The old Ianthe would most probably have talked herself out of coming here at all—but suddenly she did feel like the beautiful butterfly emerging from its chrysalis that Lysander had suggested she was when they had first met. She ached down to her very bones to be different, braver, stronger…less afraid of being hurt.

Right now she didn't want to imagine the outcome of this sizzling encounter with this amazing man. She didn't want to torture herself with consequences or barricade her heart against further pain. All Ianthe wanted to do, for the first time in her life, was let go and trust…

He didn't for one moment believe that any discussion was necessary. Not when he was deluged with a primal longing so imperative and feelings so surprising that he barely knew where to touch Ianthe first. He felt like a bear trying to gentle a lamb. This was new to Lysander, this extraordinary desire to be tender with a woman as well as fulfilling a physical need that seemed to gather momentum with each passing second. She was so pretty and appealing, with those trusting brown eyes and that plump, quivering mouth. Innocence poured out of her gaze, as well as curiosity and desire. The combination was like a perfectly spun spider's web, jewelled with early-morning dew, so delicate and enchanting that one wondered how such a thing of beauty could exist in such a relentlessly harsh world.

He decided not to answer her softly spoken question.

Instead he took her into his bedroom, letting the silence and the stillness envelop them. The task to contain his palpable need was making his muscles quiver beneath his hot, restless skin. He methodically helped her remove every piece of clothing she was wearing before finally removing his own. Lying down next to her on the bed, feeling the heat of the sun building behind the closed slats of the blind at the window, as if to echo his own rising heat, he pulled her without prevarication into his arms and kissed her.

Savouring the taste of her lush, pretty mouth, Lysander lost himself so thoroughly in the searing, sweet warmth of their kiss that it wasn't just the fulfilment of desire that drove him to hold Ianthe so possessively, but something else that beguiled him…something that hovered at the edges of his consciousness and fired little darts of shockingly pure, almost spiritual connection with her into his whole being.

He drew back from their contact, his gaze almost startled. What was he thinking? The only connection he had with the warm, receptive woman in his arms was physical. He need not dress it up by making it more complicated, and he should definitely not delude himself with imagining anything else. Because Lysander had found to his detriment that women did not always play fair. They could be both fickle and devious, and generally, he felt, were not to be trusted.

Take Marianna. She had played the part of a woman

in love so perfectly when they were first together that Lysander had convinced himself that he loved her too, had put aside his suspicions that she and his father had colluded to entice him into marriage merely to further their own aspirations. Unfortunately his suspicions had turned out to be true. Leonidas had been convinced that putting Marianna in Lysander's way was definitely in his son's best interests, because she was beautiful and accomplished and had a connection to the aristocracy. It had not mattered to him that her family had little or no money, because Leonidas believed that her royal connections would add to the gravitas of the Rosakis name. And Marianna had in her turn viewed marriage to Lysander as a source of both wealth and respectability, their official union acting as a convenient smoke-screen to hide her overly libidinous nature when it came to other men.

Lysander would not allow such a nightmare to happen again—no matter how much or how deeply he missed holding a woman close to him at night, or how tired he had become of being alone.

He smelled divine. Ianthe didn't doubt that his deeply masculine scent and the feel of those immensely strong arms of his wound possessively round her had the power to drive her close to insanity with desire. As his extraordinary eyes blazed back at her with undisguised lust, the hard and hot manifestation of that same lust brushed its full satin length tormentingly against her belly, and she let her eyes drift closed as her thighs and her hips trembled to cradle him.

She arched her spine almost clear off the bed as Lysander moved deftly above her, voraciously claiming one tightly budded nipple with the hot, silky cavern of his mouth. Ianthe could scarcely believe a body could receive this much pleasure and still live. A kitten-like mewl escaped her lips as his increasingly hungry mouth moved across to her other nipple, his teeth taunting its sensitive peak and sending spears of scalding heat knifing through her womb when he took her fully into his mouth and suckled hard. Her hands moved restlessly from the stabilising contours of his broad, smooth shoulders down his back to his waist. In the dreamlike soporific heat of the Mediterranean morning Ianthe briefly opened her eyes to find him sheathing himself with latex protection, before letting her lids naturally fall closed again and parting her thighs to welcome him inside her.

The only passing concern that surfaced briefly inside her was that she might be too tight to accept his full, commanding length into her body, because it had been so long since a man had loved her in that way. But, practically as soon as Lysander started to penetrate her, her womanly centre yielded and she let loose a surprised cry of pleasure as he deeply possessed her. Ianthe locked her fingers into the thick, blunt-cut strands of his hair, and he branded her mouth with a stirringly passionate kiss that awoke every dormant longing and need inside her with crystal-clear vitality.

He was amazing. Individually they were at opposite ends of the emotional spectrum. Lysander was confident and contained, clearly used to taking charge, his mind unhindered by doubt, and Ianthe—up until her recent decisions—was not. Yet together they seemed to complement each other…they *fitted*.

Ianthe tried very hard not to let the realisation overwhelm her. Was this what she had been missing out on all these long lonely years when she had striven to become the professional and financial success her parents aspired for her to be? Had she sacrificed the possibility of a loving relationship for material gain and security? She thought about her natural mother—loving a man who had made a baby with her she was destined not to keep—and how much joy and sorrow her union with him must have caused her. It had to have brought her unimaginable pain when she had been driven to give up her baby… Ianthe's heart almost broke at the thought.

Above her, his mesmerising visage sharply concerned, Lysander slowed his hungry possession of her body and gazed questioningly down at her. 'You are upset…why?' he demanded, his voice thick.

'Nothing. Somebody just walked over my grave, that's all.'

She touched his face with her fingers, enthralled by his fascinating bone structure, the strong, sure jaw and the compelling mouth that could deliver such devastating pleasure. The sorrow that had arisen inside her breast slowly dispersed.

'I very much like what you're doing.' The corners of her mouth edged shyly upwards. 'I don't want to talk any more. I just want you to keep making love to me.'

Lysander was glad to hear her say it. Ianthe was everything a man could desire in a woman…beautiful, sexy, intelligent, and with a sensitivity that was fiercely attractive to the things that resonated in his own soul. He didn't want to stop loving her for a long time. He trembled fiercely when he thought about how much he yearned for them both to lose themselves in the kind of deeply carnal pleasure that would allow them to keep the rest of the world at bay for a while, and, if he could dictate events at all, time would not be a factor that would impinge on his desire today…

'I will chase away any ghosts that haunt you, Ianthe,' he promised, his countenance momentarily fierce, 'and by the time I have finished making love to you, at the end of the day, there will be only one face that haunts you…and that will be *mine*.'

She'd borrowed his short towelling robe and gone to make coffee in the small undisturbed kitchen, with its cool tiled floor and plain white walls, which Ianthe was sure Lysander barely used apart from undertaking the same ordinary task that she was undertaking now. No doubt he ate out most of the time—and what urbane bachelor would want to cook for himself anyway? It made her wonder about the female influences in his life. Had his wife cooked for him? What had she been like? Did he still long to hold her as he had held Ianthe close to him all the previous day and last night—their bodies barely separate the whole night through? Ianthe was naked beneath the robe, and as the masculine scent of Lysander made provocative little asides beneath her nostrils she recalled his passionate—bordering on ferocious—lovemaking, and everything inside her throbbed and ached for his voracious possession all over again.

In the middle of spooning instant coffee granules into two mugs she stopped, to touch her burning cheeks with her palms. Polly would have barely recognised the dishevelled blushing woman standing there in that small Greek kitchen if she'd walked in now. There was nothing controlled or contained or even cautious about Ianthe this morning. She was about as undone as any woman who had spent the night exploring the many and varied joys of sex with a man who took passion to previously unimagined heights could be. And, as if to make her feel even more undone than she was already, Ianthe had made one more shocking discovery…she was in love.

What else could this mounting feeling of joy and

dread signify in her heart? She wanted to dance with happiness until she had blisters on her feet—yet at the same time she was filled with fear at the thought that she might have to walk away from Lysander without him ever knowing just how deeply and passionately she felt about him.

He walked into the kitchen wearing nothing but a pair of white cotton boxer shorts. Ianthe clenched her thighs at the disturbing and wonderful sight of him and couldn't help but blush like a self-conscious teenager.

'I'm sorry I'm taking so long making the coffee,' she apologised. Silently and, it had to be said, guiltily, she finished off the sentence in her head: *I was remembering all the delicious and naughty things we were doing last night...*

'Why don't we forget the coffee, hmm?'

To Ianthe's complete consternation, he walked up to the counter she was standing at and turned her round into his arms. As all her senses surged into tingling life Lysander parted her robe and slid his hand deftly between her thighs. Her heart began to pound with equal measures of shock and desire as she gazed into his taunting blue eyes.

'Lysander! You can't— I don't— We've got to eat! We haven't had breakfast, and I'm starving.'

'*Se thelo*, Ianthe,' he murmured.

'What does that m—?'

'I want you. *Se latrevo*. I adore you.'

'You don't fight fair!'

'Come back to bed,' he teased, unabashed, his smiling mouth and the deft, practised ministrations of his eager hands ungluing her completely. 'We will talk there about where we will go to eat and have our morning coffee. I personally know of some great places on the island that we have not visited yet.'

He taunted Ianthe further with a few short, steamy little kisses, stroked his palm across the quivering buds of her nipples, lightly pinched them, and made her sigh hungrily, feverishly, against his mouth.

'You are a very wicked man, and I'm sure that you know it,' she murmured as he lifted her effortlessly into his arms and strode with obvious licentious purpose back into the bedroom.

'You are aware that these days "wicked" means good?' he drawled. 'So I will take your accusation as a compliment, and gladly give you another demonstration of just how wicked I can be.'

Laughing huskily, Lysander lowered her to the bed and swiftly joined her…

It came to him quite clearly what he should do about the dinner party back home in Athens. Oh, he still intended to go—he would not deliberately disappoint his beloved mother for anything—but Lysander had every intention of taking along a guest with him. Ianthe. Not only would it satisfy his own insatiable need to have her with him, it would also show his father once and for all that his son was never going to be manipulated into a relationship of his father's choosing again. If Leonidas proved to be angry or embarrassed that Lysander had brought an unexpected female guest to the little soirée he had arranged with his friend and his daughter, then it would be his own arrogant fault anyway. How *dared* he believe that he could still command the direction of his son's life for him, even after Lysander's disastrous union with Marianna?

As they arrived at the entrance to the small hotel Ianthe was staying at, with the scent of the honeysuckle and magnolia prevalent in the courtyard hypnotically filling the air, Lysander once again impelled her into his arms. Her eyes were bright and liquid, dark with expectation, and she looked like a woman who had spent a day and a night and half the next morning in the arms of her very enamoured lover. His blood quickened restlessly at the flood of memories that ensued. They rose up to torment him with merciless emphasis, in case he should forget for even a second that she had given him a glimpse of paradise he wouldn't soon forget, and he realised that he did not want to let her go—not even for a few short hours to write her postcards home, wash her hair and get ready to meet him again later on this afternoon.

'I did not tell you where I was taking you tonight?' He smiled, pausing to extricate a tiny white feather that had obviously worked loose from his pillow and lodged itself in the rich chocolate strands of her hair. Ianthe stared transfixed at the feather and silently shook her head in wonderment—as if she too had suddenly been explicitly visited by an erotic recollection of their many passionate hours together.

'Where are you taking me tonight?' she asked softly, her lips curving sweetly as she rested her hands lightly on the small of Lysander's back.

'To my parents' home in Athens. They are throwing a small dinner party that I promised I would attend, and I thought it might be very pleasant if you came with me.'

Registering the word 'parents', Ianthe couldn't deny the throb of unease that momentarily upset her equilibrium. She was in unchartered waters here, with no guidance as to how to best respond. She didn't want to make a big deal about the unexpected invitation, yet at the same time she couldn't deny she was disturbed by it.

'You want us to go back to Athens…tonight?' she asked, letting her hands rest loosely on his hips now.

'My father is sending a boat.'

'A *boat*?'

'A yacht, then.' Lysander shrugged, as though the concept was totally ordinary and unimportant, barely even worthy of comment.

Ianthe frowned and pulled her hands free completely. 'I don't understand…your father has a yacht?'

'Many wealthy Greeks have yachts, Ianthe. You have

seen some of them lined up here in the harbour. It is really not so astonishing.'

The invitation to Athens to have dinner with Lysander's parents took on a whole new worrying aspect. She had had no idea that background he came from included the kind of wealth that meant a yacht, and parents who would send it to pick up their son just so that he could attend a dinner party. How on earth would they react when they found out that their handsome, no doubt highly eligible son had brought along an ordinary English girl who was on holiday on the island to join them for dinner? An outsider?

'I—I had no idea that your family were wealthy, Lysander.'

'Why would you?' His gaze was momentarily troubled. 'I never discussed it with you. Does it bother you that my family have money?'

He too dropped his hands to his sides and seemed preoccupied with thoughts unspoken.

'It doesn't *bother* me as such, but it does make me feel a little uneasy, if I'm honest. And I don't understand why you are asking me to come and meet them. We haven't known each other long, and it seems—it seems inappropriate, somehow.'

Lysander stared broodingly at Ianthe. He admired the fact that she seemed to have reservations about meeting his family when they had only just met—it was a very different response from that most other women he took out would have, and it reassured him that it was *he* that she was interested in, not the fact that he came from money. Yet at the same time he was perversely irritated by her reluctance. He had invited her to go to dinner with his family and, as far as he was concerned, that was all the reason she needed to accept.

'I am not taking you home with me as my prospective wife, Ianthe. I have merely had an invitation to dinner and have asked you to accompany me. It is as simple as that. There is no need to make it more complicated.'

Suddenly the invitation to dinner seemed even less inviting than before. To Ianthe's sensitive hearing it sounded as if Lysander was slightly embarrassed and irritated by the doubts she had expressed—as though he believed she had somehow read much more into the invitation than he'd meant.

I am not taking you home with me as my prospective wife, he'd assured her, and Ianthe felt the cutting slice of every one of those well-aimed words as though they had physically pierced her skin. It had not crossed her mind for even one second that she could ever be his wife…had it? Just because she found herself swept away by feelings of love it didn't mean that she wanted to rush headlong into marriage. How dared Lysander arrogantly assume that she would even entertain such an idea?

'I'm not trying to complicate anything, Lysander, I can assure you. All things considered, I think I'll decline the invitation, if you don't mind. We've spent quite a bit of time together and I probably could do with some time on my own. You go and enjoy your dinner, and perhaps I'll see you around in a couple of days or so?'

He could not believe she was being so cool with him—so curt. Lysander felt a muscle quiver in the side of his cheek.

'I *want* you to come to Athens with me! If I had planned on taking you to a restaurant on the island tonight you would have come with me—yes?'

'Yes, but—'

'So there is no need to change our plans to have dinner together just because the venue has changed. I very much want you to come with me tonight, Ianthe. If my manner was less than inviting before, then I apologise. I promise I will make it up to you.'

Even though his apology sounded more annoyed than conciliatory, Ianthe felt her heart kick up at the very appealing smile flirting around the edges of his compelling lips. She wanted to be with him tonight, too…no matter where that would be. Their dinner-date might work out okay, or it might be a disaster, but at the end of the day it wasn't Lysander's parents whose company she yearned for. It was their son's—and right now he was unashamedly devouring her, driving her clear out of her mind with the wicked desire that shone lasciviously from his impossibly blue eyes…

CHAPTER SEVEN

IANTHE had just about recovered from her surprise at the sheer size and beauty of Lysander's father's yacht, which had been waiting for them to board at the harbour and taken them into the nearest port, when she was shocked again by the luxurious chauffeur-driven limo that drove them into the city.

She tried to stuff her trepidation deep down inside her as they were shown into the stunning formal drawing room of his parents' house in a wealthy suburb of Athens. They had been escorted to the room, with its array of original art hanging on the walls and its opulent furniture and furnishings that unashamedly displayed their quality and exclusivity, by an unctuous manservant. Ianthe had barely been able to glance at Lysander, she had been so nervous and intimidated.

This was a very different background from the one Ianthe was certain her poor mother must have inhabited growing up. No doubt it had helped Lysander immensely to develop his career as a photographer, knowing that he didn't have to struggle to make ends meet.

She bit back the uncharitable thought, guiltily remembering her own parents' financial assistance and support in helping her establish *her* business. There was nothing wrong with a little family support. Yet at the same time she couldn't help feeling uneasy at the idea that Lysander hailed from money—and not just common or garden wealth but the kind of fabulous riches that most people could only wonder at. Right now she didn't quite know how to deal with that. It was one thing enjoying the freedom of being with each other on the island, where nobody else was involved, but her relationship with him was taking on a whole new complexion now that she could see where he came from.

Glancing at the slender dark-haired beauty beside him in her black satin strapless cocktail dress, her smooth, lightly tanned shoulders draped with a light fringed shawl of midnight-blue, Lysander couldn't deny the spurt of pride and possession that shot through him.

He knew if his mother Galatea got to know Ianthe she would not be able to help but love her, and the thought gave him a moment's untroubled pleasure—before his father walked into the room in his dinner suit and trampled the little oasis of calm with all the force and presence of a Sherman tank. His dark eyes scanned the well-dressed young couple standing amid the splendour of his drawing room with piercing examination.

Lysander knew whatever transpired next would undoubtedly set the tone for the rest of the evening. He deliberately settled an air of challenge across his shoulders. Let the old trickster do his worst! He was not going to allow Ianthe to be upset, though, and nor would he be drawn into a confrontation—not this time. If the old man played up too much, he would simply take Ianthe by the hand and leave. He would book them both into a nice hotel and then in the morning they would travel back to the island.

He inclined his head briefly in greeting to Leonidas. *'Kalispera,* Father.'

'You have brought a guest, I see, Lysander. Why did you not let your mother know?'

Ianthe detected straight away that something was amiss, even though the big man spoke in Greek. She was not welcome here. So why had Lysander insisted on her accompanying him? Next to her, he raised one broad, suited shoulder in a shrug, but underneath that apparently relaxed gesture she sensed surprising anger. She swallowed hard, wishing she had been more insistent in telling him that she would prefer not to come with him on this particular dinner-date.

'You can speak in English, Father. My friend is not familiar with the Greek language. Are you suggesting that you cannot accommodate us both?' he demanded. 'If that is the case, then naturally we will leave.'

He captured her hand in his and gripped it. Ianthe glanced up at him in alarm and concern. Clearly the two men did not enjoy the easiest of relationships, if this tense little exchange was anything to judge by, and she wondered at the cause of the animosity between them.

'Lysander—my dear son!' Immediately remorseful, the commanding man who was his father strode across the room and gripped Lysander reassuringly by the shoulder, at the same time bestowing a smile of startling wattage upon Ianthe. 'What nonsense is this you are speaking? As if we could not accommodate a beautiful guest of our son's! I was merely pointing out that your mother was not aware that she needed to arrange for another place to be set at dinner. But that can be accomplished with not a moment's trouble, so do not be concerned…either of you. Perhaps, Lysander, you would do me the honour of introducing me to your guest?'

Stepping slightly away from his father, Lysander let go of Ianthe's hand and looked very serious as he glanced first at Leonidas, then at his companion. 'This is Ianthe. We have been spending some time together on the island. Ianthe, this is my father—Leonidas Rosakis.'

'Ianthe?' Leonidas frowned. 'That is a very Greek name! Yet apparently you are not Greek?' He addressed her quizzically.

'No, I'm from England…London.' Once again Ianthe

experienced a flash of guilt and embarrassment as she avoided explaining her true origins. Every time she denied her ancestry, or spoke as though she had no knowledge of it, she felt somehow that she was betraying her real mother. Betraying the pain and fear she must have gone through when she was forced to abandon her baby.

She smiled a little nervously as Leonidas firmly gripped her hand, his gaze perusing her blushing countenance a little too closely for comfort.

'Well, you are very welcome in my house, Ianthe. Now, you must both come and meet our other guests.'

As they entered the stunning dining room Ianthe saw three people already there. An attractive middle-aged woman in a fitted ivory dress that displayed her still admirable figure, a portly man of around the same age, nursing what looked to be a glass of Scotch, and a young, gorgeous dark-blonde beauty with a daringly low backless emerald evening gown. The trio all stood examining a large oil painting of an impressive ship at sea.

They turned at Leonidas's booming voice, all smiles—until their eyes settled upon Ianthe. Once again she found herself wondering why Lysander had brought her to his family's home when her unexpected presence was clearly about as welcome as smallpox.

Recovering first, the woman who Ianthe immediately assumed to be Lysander's mother rushed forward and embraced her son. This time Lysander did not visibly stiffen, as he had done when his father's hand had clamped down upon his shoulder, but instead his hands rested easily at his mother's waist as he kissed her warmly on both cheeks.

'You look as beautiful as ever, Mother,' he told her affectionately, then stood back to admire her.

'Galatea, my dear, Lysander has brought a friend with him tonight. Her name is Ianthe—but she is definitely not Greek, he tells me!' Leonidas made the announcement loudly, then laughed as if enjoying a great joke.

Ianthe sensed the undercurrent of irritation and disappointment beneath that supposedly relaxed laugh. If her presence was going to cause trouble between Lysander and his family, then she would rather just leave now than sit with them at dinner and endure what could only be sheer agony.

She gripped her black satin evening purse more tightly between her hands as her gaze touched briefly on the other two guests. The beautiful young woman in the eye-catching emerald gown that clung to her slender body like dew to the petal of a flower flicked a clearly annoyed glance back at Ianthe, then turned, all her interest on Lysander. It was very obvious who her particular attention was going to be reserved for, and Ianthe couldn't suppress the nauseating flare of jealousy that immediately unsettled her stomach. Was that why they were all so upset with her being there? she wondered suddenly. Because this gorgeous vision in emerald green had been waiting to be introduced to Lysander?

'*Kalosorisate,* Ianthe. Welcome.'

Lysander's attractive mother pressed her hand across Ianthe's, where it held her purse in a death grip, and smiled. There was neither disappointment nor regret in that completely genuine gesture, and Ianthe sensed a little of her tension disperse.

'Forgive our being so unprepared to greet you, but we had no idea Lysander was bringing a friend. However, I want you to know that you are *most* welcome in my house. Please come and meet our other guests—Takis Koumanidis and his lovely daughter Electra. They have both been eagerly waiting to meet Lysander.'

Takis stepped forward and warmly shook Lysander's hand, then stepped back to allow his daughter to do the same. She couldn't take her eyes off of him, and she put her hand deliberately on the immaculate tailoring of his dinner jacket sleeve and let it possessively linger there. Ianthe felt her body grow tense all over again at the other woman's predatory stance.

Lysander, for his part, did not appear particularly impressed or enamoured of the woman. As soon as the introductions had been made he turned to Ianthe and placed his hand at her back. A series of explosive tingles spread out across her spine as she recalled how passionately they had been engaged with each other only a few short hours ago. She longed to be back in his bed, beneath the shelter of that simple little whitewashed house next to the ocean—not here, in this veritable palace!

They would not linger at the dinner party, Lysander determined as they moved to sit at the long, beautifully laid table. A place for Ianthe was hastily yet tactfully set next to his by another quickly summoned manservant, and Electra was reluctantly forced to take the place opposite them. He slid his hand onto Ianthe's thigh beneath her satin dress and would almost swear that he felt the heat between them burn through the material. His blue eyes darkened with predatory hunger as he turned to survey the answering flush that had tinted her lovely cheeks at his touch.

He wanted to whisper in her ear that he could not wait to take her back to the island again, back to his bed, so much so that he was going to fall into a fever if he could not do it soon—but it was time for him to pour the wine for Electra and Ianthe, and he had to try and contain the storm of lust that swept through his body like a heady sirocco.

'So…Ianthe.' Seated next to his daughter, Takis Koumanidis raised his wine glass to his lips and seemed to study Ianthe hard. 'Tell us, please, what brings you to Greece and where are you from?'

Taken aback by the unexpectedly probing quality of the question, Ianthe nervously licked her lips before replying. 'I'm here on holiday, from London. That's where I live. This is my first visit to your country. I've always wanted to come to Greece…and now I have,' she finished awkwardly.

'And what do you do for a living back in London?' Takis enquired as he broke the bread on his side-plate but did not eat it.

'What do I do for a living? Well, I…' She glanced sidelong at Lysander, who was not hiding his own interest in her answer. 'I used to own a business, but I've recently put it up for sale.'

'It was not going well?' Her interrogator's beetle-black brows came momentarily together with razor-sharp curiosity.

Ianthe sighed and spread her white linen napkin carefully on her lap. 'It was going very well, as a matter of fact, but I could no longer find the interest in it that I used to. I decided I needed a new direction.'

She hoped that would be explanation enough. She was still too tender about Polly, and about the personal family revelations she had uncovered, to discuss any of it with other people—let alone strangers.

'And what is it that you intend to do, now that you have given it up?' Takis persisted.

Uncomfortable with both the question and the attention she seemed to be commanding, Ianthe reached for her glass of wine and took a gulp. The alcohol careened helpfully through her veins and, after stealing another sidelong glance at Lysander, she forced herself to come up with an answer. 'I thought I might travel a little. I haven't really been anywhere very much, and I would like to see a bit more of the world.'

She sensed her listeners' immediate loss of interest in her as she disclosed her apparent lack of ambition. Clearly they didn't understand it at all. In their minds they obviously had her down as a quitter for selling her business and giving it up. She couldn't help speculating as to what Lysander must think of her casual admission of future intent. Did he think she was lazy to make such a choice instead of pursuing another lucrative career? It made her wonder why people always seemed to be judged on what they did for a living rather than the kind of person they were. Wasn't it enough just to be a decent human being? In Ianthe's opinion that was about as good a definition of success as anything. Obviously, going by all the material wealth surrounding her, Lysander's family thought differently.

'And you, Lysander…' Takis beetled his brows at the man seated next to Ianthe, as if he was at last getting round to the person he'd really come to see. 'How long are you on vacation for? I hear from Leonidas that you have been busy with your photography whilst you have been away, but business is important too, no? When are you coming back to work? I have a very interesting proposition to put to you as soon as you return.'

Electra seemed to preen herself as her father finished speaking, and gazed pointedly at Lysander, as if defying him not to enjoy her beauty and desire her. Realising that she was probably of no further interest to the people seated around the table—with the exception of her lover—Ianthe fiddled with her napkin and wished she was anywhere else in the world but seated here, in this intimidatingly lovely dining room, with a group of people she had not one thing in common with and most likely never would.

But then she suddenly registered Takis's comments and the full implication of them began to sink in. What did he mean by 'business is important too'? And 'when are you coming back to work'? Lysander worked as a photographer for a living...hadn't he told her as much when they'd first met? Her dark eyes were puzzled as they turned to study him, but his astonishingly captivating profile was right now an impenetrable mask that effectively hid whatever might be on his mind from prying onlookers.

She began to feel very uneasy.

'I will come back to work when I am ready, and not before. I regret that your proposition will have to wait. Right now, I am afraid that my vacation is taking precedence over anything else. I have earned it, so why should it not?'

'Of course he has earned it!' Galatea pronounced on her son's behalf. 'What is the good of being head of a company if you cannot delegate responsibility to others when you need a break? Rosakis Shipping may have dominated the life of my husband, but Lysander is still young; it is only natural that he should be interested in other pursuits as well as the family business! When is Christophe arranging the exhibition for you, my dear? I want to make sure that I bring all my friends.'

So Lysander was head of the family business...and that business was Rosakis Shipping.

No wonder his father had a yacht the size of a small mansion. He probably had several others as well! And surely being head of such an illustrious and wealthy business meant that Lysander was independently wealthy as well...a millionaire, even?

Ianthe glanced at her handsome companion with shock flooding her insides. From the moment she'd stepped inside this astonishingly opulent room and sat down at the beautifully laid table with these wealthy, fabulously attired people, she had not believed she could eat a thing. And after hearing this most recent revelation about Lysander—the man she had fallen in love with—if she attempted to put food into her mouth at all she would most likely choke on it!

Why had he kept his true identity secret from her? Didn't she merit the truth? Did he think that she might be some sort of gold-digger?

'Let us enjoy some wine before our meal,' Leonidas announced at the head of the table, raising his glass high. 'There will be plenty of time afterwards to discuss matters of business if we so wish. Besides, there are ladies present—and very beautiful ladies too! We are very fortunate indeed to have their company, are we not?'

As they stepped off his father's yacht into the balmy Greek night back on the island, Lysander glanced at the silent young woman by his side and felt his insides clench in concern. Ianthe had barely said a word to him on the journey back, and he had to know the reason for her sudden coolness towards him.

It had not been one of the most enjoyable or successful dinner parties he had ever attended, and at times the atmosphere had been almost impossibly stultifying. If it had not been for Galatea, practically begging him to be there for her sake as well as his father's, Lysander would have had no compunction in refusing the invitation flatly. Now, looking at Ianthe's pale, preoccupied face, he really wished that he had. Leonidas had done his very best to push the man-eating Electra Koumanidis towards him all evening, even steering Ianthe towards Takis several times, to get her to converse with him rather than Lysander. He couldn't deny he had felt almost savagely jealous about the other man's obvious interest in Ianthe. The old goat had monopolised her as though he could not get enough of her company. What on earth did his father think he was playing at now?

He saw Ianthe shiver suddenly beneath her flimsy blue wrap and it shook him out of his painful little reverie. 'You are cold. Here, let me give you my jacket.'

But as he started to remove the beautifully tailored dinner jacket Ianthe shook her head firmly in protest. 'No, don't do that. I'm fine, really.'

They started to walk away from the harbour, with its twinkling lights strung alongside the luxurious yachts moored there. Lysander simply had to know why Ianthe was suddenly—deliberately, it seemed—distancing herself from him. As she turned towards the direction of the road that led to her hotel he fastened his fingers possessively around the top of her arm.

'No. Not that way.'

He didn't want her to go back to the hotel tonight. He wanted her in his bed...where she belonged.

As well as his grip on her arm, the command in his voice was obvious. Ianthe could no longer contain the fury that had been simmering inside her all evening.

'Why not? That's where my hotel is!'

She wrenched her arm free from his hold and stepped away from him, breathing hard. Lysander's disturbingly blue eyes reflected his surprise and shock.

'All right—are you going to tell me what is making you so angry with me tonight? If anyone has a right to be angry, it's me! You spent most of the evening flirting with that obnoxious little man Takis Koumanidis!'

Ianthe's knees almost crumpled in surprise. 'I was not flirting with him one little bit! Are you crazy? It's *you* that spent half the night gazing down Electra's sleazily low neckline! If anyone has a right to be furious it's me! But it's not that, Lysander.' She gulped, dark eyes helplessly glittering with unshed tears. 'It's worse than that. You lied to me.'

CHAPTER EIGHT

'LIED to you?'

Ianthe could see straight away that he didn't understand. That upset her even more. Was she so unimportant to him that he couldn't even remember that he had told her he worked as a photographer for his living? Not as the head of a doubtless multimillion-dollar shipping company!

Perhaps this was the wake-up call that she needed, to help her come to her senses and make her see that Lysander was simply playing with her—*using* her—to help pass some time whilst he was on vacation. To think that she was anything more to him than a holiday fling was simply being naïve. A slow tear tracked its way down her cheek and she wiped it away impatiently, furious with herself for giving way to emotion in front of a man who clearly was not worth the heartache.

'You said you were a photographer. You led me to believe that was how you worked for your living. Never at any point did you correct me in that assumption. You *lied* to me, Lysander! Do you really expect me to believe that you somehow *forgot* to tell me what you really do? You're the head of a wealthy shipping business, your family are so rich they can send a huge great luxury yacht to take you to Athens just for a dinner party, and you didn't even mention it!'

His handsome face looked pensive but not unduly concerned at her outburst. 'I may not have told you the whole truth about what I do, Ianthe, but you didn't need to know. Does it matter? After all, you never asked me to elaborate. And in any case, what are you getting so worked up about? Do you honestly expect me to believe that the fact that I am wealthy is a problem for you? You would be a rare woman amongst your sex if that was the case. It's usually the other way around.' He shrugged, smiling, and Ianthe itched to wipe the clear evidence of his impossible arrogance right off his too-confident face.

'Some of us have principles!'

Raising her anguished gaze to his, Ianthe hugged her flimsy wrap across her chest and wished this crushing sense of disappointment and betrayal would just go away and leave her alone. She wished she could have fooled herself for a little while longer that she really had found something very special with this man. It was now clear to her that he thought very differently about their affair.

'Not all women are impressed by wealth for its own sake,' she told him bitterly. 'It was you I was attracted to, Lysander, not your bank balance, so you didn't need to hide it. Some of us think that not deceiving people is a lot more important than whether you have money or not! And if you're suggesting I would want to be with you for the sake of your money, that's an insult. As though I'd just been using you for your wealth! It must have been a very lonely existence for you if that's been your experience with women so far.'

Her words cut into him like acid burns. They reminded him of his tortured marriage to Marianna—indeed, they reminded him of the loneliness he had endured right up until her shocking death. Because she had indeed used him. She'd played him like a prize fool and stupidly he had fallen for her avid declarations of love and let them blind him to the truth.

Now he knew that it was infinitely better to be on one's own than in a relationship that day after day chipped little parts of your soul away. Only the prospect of having a child had kept him trying to make that mendacious, loveless marriage work. But at the end of the day even that had been cruelly wrenched from his grasp...

'I *am* a photographer, Ianthe. I did not lie to you about that. You saw my photographs in the gallery. Just because I am head of my family's business does not mean that I cannot pursue other passions in my life...and photography *is* my passion. We have not talked very much about ourselves, have we? Perhaps the truth is we have both been keeping secrets from each other?'

'I have not kept secrets from you! Not big ones,

about who I really am!' she protested angrily. But even as she articulated the words she knew they weren't exactly true. Thinking about the real reason she had fled to Greece, to this island, the quest she hadn't mentioned to anyone, Ianthe was silently stung by the painful accuracy of Lysander's words.

But the secret of her birth wasn't relevant—and it was nothing compared to his concealment of his wealth! Ianthe could not get past her hurt or anger that yet another person in her life—someone she had really grown to care for—had deliberately lied to her. She was starting to believe that she must have some secret sign emblazoned upon her forehead that read: *Do not tell this woman the truth—she is not strong enough to withstand it.*

She sighed into the night, with its exotic tang of heat and foreign oceans and a totally different way of life from the one she knew back home, and suddenly felt a real wrench of her soul. She wanted to be back again in England, amongst the people she knew really loved her.

She recalled the sour, unhappy note on which she had left home. Her anger at the fact that her parents had lied to her about her true origins. Her mother's distress. The way the words, 'We'll always love you, Ianthe, no matter where you go!' had followed her as she'd slammed out through the door of their house in a temper. Suddenly she felt so distraught that she could barely contain her anguish.

'I want to go back to the hotel now,' she said quietly,

her gaze deliberately avoiding Lysander's. 'It's been a long evening and I'm very tired.'

'If that is your wish, then I will walk you back there. Tomorrow we can meet up again and—'

'No. I need some time, Lysander. I don't think it's a good idea if we meet again for a while. Please understand.'

Lysander bit back his angry protest—only because he could see Ianthe was already distressed. But how on earth was he supposed to understand her need to stay away from him for a while, when he still could not fully comprehend why she was so upset with him? It was enough to test his restraint to the maximum! He accepted that she had principles—the fact that she would not have associated with him for gain because of his wealth and her integrity had certainly struck a satisfied chord deep with him, and after Marianna's cheating ways, how could it not?—but Ianthe was simply erecting barriers where they need not be if she insisted on viewing his occupation and background as some kind of black mark against him.

Was she seriously thinking of ending their affair because he was rich? Lysander wanted to curse out loud until his vocal cords would not let him curse any more. Since they had made love he had developed certain... *feelings* for this woman. Feelings he was almost too scared to explore in any depth, yet which were strong enough and commanding enough not to be ignored.

He didn't want it to be over yet.

Reluctantly he walked her back to the entrance of the hotel where she was staying—unable to help, wishing he were facing a very different scenario than the one that now confronted him—and tried to swallow his pride when she turned her head away from him and would not let him kiss her goodnight.

Shaking out two headache pills into her hand from the crumpled box in her purse, Ianthe swallowed them down with a large gulp of water and grimaced at her wan reflection in the bathroom mirror. She'd definitely looked better.

It was late morning, and she had slept in because she had not been able to fall asleep until the early hours. The events of the evening had played over and over again in her mind with relentless repetition, the characters that had dominated it flashing through her brain like taunting ghosts. Now her head felt as hot as the desert—complete with a herd of camels pounding through it—and it was only through sheer strength of will that she stopped herself from giving way to the tears that were pressing avidly behind her eyelids.

Why hadn't Lysander been able to trust her with the truth about what he did? If he had, she would still have felt the same about him…wouldn't she?

But even as she speculated on her answer she had to silently confess that she'd been much enamoured of the romantic notion that he was a simple photographer, with a free and easy lifestyle that allowed him to travel at will and take his photographs...a free spirit. She'd dreamed that maybe he came from a very ordinary Greek family who loved him dearly and were immensely proud of his achievements. A family he might have introduced Ianthe to, given time; a family who might have helped to fill the void of yearning inside her to know her birth family.

Instead Lysander had introduced her to practically the equivalent of the British Royal Family! There was nothing simple about Lysander Rosakis's life—Ianthe could see that a mile away. There was a weight of expectation and demand directed towards him—a weight of obligation from and to his wealthy family. Why would he have a vain, sullen creature like Electra Koumanidis paraded in front of him if not for the purpose of possibly uniting two illustrious families in marriage? Takis Koumanidis had not spared Ianthe the details of his family's impressive connections and lineage, and the more she had listened to him speak, the less she had been inclined to tell him anything about herself. When he had started talking loudly about how his beautiful daughter was just a 'simple homemaker' at heart—a girl who longed for a husband and family to make her life complete—Ianthe had realised she was being warned off, that both families were nursing very real hopes that Lysander and Electra might get together.

Ianthe had torn her gaze away from Takis's intense dark stare to seek out the man who occupied most of her waking thoughts—and had found her lover apparently absorbed in whatever the predatory Electra was saying to him. If she could have sprouted a pair of wings she would have flown back to the island right there and then—but instead she'd had to endure several more awkward hours before she and Lysander were finally able to make their goodbyes and leave.

Now, in spite of her hurt and dismay over the fact that he'd lied to her about his real occupation, and the horrible possibility that if he could lie about that then he could lie about anything else, Ianthe couldn't help but long to be back in his arms again. Call her weak, misguided, all the things she strove not to be, but it was hard to fight such powerful feelings of overwhelming need. All she wanted to do was shut out the rest of the world and just bask in the feeling of his strong, protective arms around her, making her feel loved. Even though he clearly didn't love her at all…

The phone on her bedside table rang, shattering the relative quiet. Still gazing into the mirror, she saw hope flare in her eyes that it might be Lysander calling. She rushed back into the bedroom and practically tore the receiver from its rest.

'Hello?'

'Miss Dane?' returned the receptionist's rather serious tones from down in the lobby. 'You have a visitor who wishes to see you. Can you come down?'

Who else could it be but Lysander? Maybe he'd come

to apologise? Maybe he'd had good reason for not telling her the truth about what he did for a living and now he wanted to explain. She could at least hear him out, couldn't she? The logical part of her brain told her that she was like all women in love—blind to the faults of her lover—but Ianthe didn't want to even go there. All she wanted to do right now was see the face of the man she loved. The man she needed.

Scraping back her hair from her forehead with suddenly impatient fingers, Ianthe did not hesitate to give her answer. 'I'll come down directly.'

But when she arrived in the high-ceilinged lobby, with its chequered marble floor, this time wearing rubber-soled sandals that hardly made any sound at all against the stone, attired in a pink summer dress whose narrow straps prettily displayed her newly tanned shoulders, it was to find not Lysander but a formally suited Takis Koumanidis.

Swallowing down bitter disappointment, and barely able to hear her own voice above the sonorous thud of her heartbeat, Ianthe prayed the older man couldn't tell that she was clearly expecting to see Lysander.

'Mr Koumanidis? This is a surprise.'

'*Kalimera,* Ianthe. Please forgive my intrusion on your plans for the day, but I was hoping that you could spare me half an hour or so to come and have coffee with me?'

Scarcely knowing what to think about such an unexpected and surprising invitation, Ianthe smoothed her hands nervously down her dress. Then a shocking thought occurred. Had he come here to warn her to keep away from Lysander so that the way would be free for his daughter to make her move?

Swallowing down her resentment and hurt, Ianthe forced herself to remain calm. 'Is something the matter, Mr Koumanidis?'

Briefly examining the thick gold band on his marriage finger, he dropped his hand to his side and smiled at her, displaying very even white teeth that were clearly expensively capped. 'Please—call me Takis. There is nothing for you to be alarmed about, my dear. I simply want to have a little chat with you. Will you do me the honour?'

Unable to come up with a good reason to refuse him, Ianthe inclined her head reluctantly. 'Okay…'

'You know, when I first saw you, my dear, I had quite a shock.'

Pensively stirring his coffee at the café table, Takis raised his almost black deep-set eyes to Ianthe and seemed to study her with all the intense scrutiny of a witness to a crime examining a police line-up. It made Ianthe more than a little uneasy—especially when she was still none the wiser about what he wanted to have a 'little chat' with her for.

'Oh? Why was that?'

'You are practically the living image of someone I used to know,' Takis confessed with a deep sigh.

Ianthe frowned, waiting for him to explain.

'Her name was Ianthe too. She was just eighteen when we became lovers and I was twenty-four. That was over thirty years ago. The next part is not easy to say out loud, but I will try.'

Paying no attention to her own cup of coffee, Ianthe could scarcely take her eyes off of Takis.

Withdrawing a perfectly white handkerchief from his inside jacket pocket, he mopped his perspiring brow before continuing. 'I told you last night a little of the history of my forebears. My family made their fortune a long time ago. We are—how do you put it?—old money. Ianthe's family were a different story. They were poor—*very* poor. We would definitely not have been considered a good match. Add to that the fact that her family were very religious—almost fanatically so—and mine were not, you can see that the odds of continuing our relationship were firmly against us. But still, if I had had the strength to go against the demands of my father I would have married her when she became pregnant with my child.'

He paused to shake his head and Ianthe almost thought she saw moisture glinting in his expressive dark eyes. Her heartbeat slowed and all her blood seemed to swim straight to her head. 'What did—what did you do?' she asked, her mouth so dry that her words did not have an easy passage.

'I gave her the money to travel to England and have an abortion.'

'And—and did she?'

By now Ianthe was twisting her hands together on the table in front of her, her face growing paler by the second. Thirty years ago they'd had the affair, he'd said...so Ianthe would be the right age.

The man opposite her once more mopped his brow with the voluminous handkerchief. 'I never heard of or saw my sweet Ianthe again, so I cannot tell you the answer to that. I told myself that she must have met some man in England, perhaps married him and settled down there. There is not a day that goes past when I do not think of her. When you walked into my friend's house with his son last night I could hardly believe my eyes. You look so much like her that it is almost frightening. Even the way you smile and move is like her! I could not sleep for wondering. Who are your parents, Ianthe?' he asked almost hungrily. 'Do they have a connection with my country, perhaps?'

'My parents are both English,' she heard herself reply, while inside nothing less than mayhem reigned—as though someone had thrown a handgrenade into a previously tidy room and devastated it. 'My mother's from Sussex and my father's a Yorkshire man. My grandparents were all English too, and as far as I know so were their parents. I'm sorry I can't tell you any more than that, Mr Koumanidis.'

'I see. I apologise for burdening you with my sad story, Ianthe, but I hope that you can understand why I had to tell you—had to ask?'

'Astonishing coincidences happen all the time.' Ianthe shrugged, smiled, then tentatively—because her hand was shaking—lifted her cup of coffee to her lips and sipped. 'I am sorry if my appearance stirred old wounds. I am sure that wherever your Ianthe is now, she is well and happy. Perhaps some memories are best left alone, don't you think?'

For a moment their gazes met and held, then Ianthe looked quickly away again, unable to deal with the disappointed hope and at the same time the relief that she saw in his. Her breath was so tight in her chest she could scarcely breathe. She needed to be away from crowds, she realised, glancing around at the other diners, innocently enjoying the day. She needed to be far away from people. What Takis Koumanidis had just revealed to her was just too much to take in all at once. She needed to be alone.

CHAPTER NINE

LYSANDER finally resorted to the one thing that might provide the distraction he needed from the avalanche of frustration and ire that plagued him. Collecting his camera, a bag of fruit and a bottle of water, he stuffed them all into a knapsack, swung it onto his shoulder and left the little house that hugged the harbour to its own devices for the day.

He headed along the dusty unmade road into the main street of the little town, intending to pay a visit to his friend Ari's gallery before walking off into the hills to take some scenic photographs.

Doing something physical as well as utilising his camera skills would hopefully keep his increasingly in-cessant desire to see Ianthe again if not at bay, then at least simmering manageably beneath the surface. She'd said she'd needed some time before seeing him again. How much time did she mean? A day? A week? Longer than that? Would he see her at all before she finally travelled back to England?

Silently cursing his inability to put her completely out of his mind, Lysander deliberately increased his stride in the hope that his physical exertion might somehow outpace his thoughts.

He swung by a particularly elegant little café that was often monopolised by some of the wealthy Athenians he was acquainted with—and his footsteps ground almost to a halt as he saw Takis Koumanidis, his father's 'old friend', with Ianthe. As he watched they rose up together from the table they'd been sitting at, and Takis affectionately kissed Ianthe on both cheeks.

Disbelief vied with a fury that was corrosive, and it was like thunder raging inside him. Sweat cleaved to his back as heat assailed his whole body and almost physically made him see red. His suspicions about the avid interest Takis had taken in Ianthe last night at his parents' house were apparently no fantasy. The man was making a play for her right under Lysander's nose! He had naturally assumed his father's friend was married—he'd noticed a wedding band on the man's finger—but clearly he was not averse to having mistresses, and he intended Ianthe to be the next one.

He watched her run down the wide, curved stone steps that led back onto the road, her dark hair swinging freely down her back, in a pink summer dress, and Lysander did not hesitate to follow her. He waited until she'd turned into the narrow little road that led back to her hotel before sprinting to catch up with her. Too furious to be polite, he grabbed her arm and pulled her forcefully against his chest.

He saw fear, then recognition, then puzzlement swirl into her surprised dark gaze, and for a moment he was intoxicated by the sight of her small elegant features so close to his once again. But then he remembered that she was more than likely about to cheat on him—despite her so-called principles!—and his anger almost choked him.

'What were you doing with Takis Koumanidis? Answer me!'

It was like being suddenly hurled into the eye of a violent storm. One moment Ianthe had been walking innocently along, intent on getting quickly back to her hotel room to absorb the startling revelations Takis had made known to her in private, and then she'd been suddenly, almost roughly manhandled and hauled up against her lover's chest in the middle of the street!

She realised that the Greek style of expression sometimes led to public displays of emotion—but it was still an almighty shock to be confronted by Lysander like this, so openly, beneath the unapologetic stares of passers by.

'Let go of me! Lysander—what's wrong with you?'

She tried to wrench her arm free. He let it go unexpectedly, when she wasn't prepared, and one foot slid awkwardly against the shiny stone of the street as she almost lost her balance.

'What about your famous principles now, Ianthe? Tell me that! What did you think you were doing, taking coffee with my father's friend? Exchanging investment tips, perhaps?' His expression was brutally derogatory. 'Is he the reason that you told me last night you needed some time before seeing me again? What has he done—made you an offer you cannot refuse?'

As the meaning of the furious words he flung at her began to penetrate her understanding, Ianthe felt her legs turn to rubber. Her dark eyes stinging with disbelief, she stared at him, then laid her hand protectively over the place where his fingers had gripped her too tightly, her resentment growing.

'You don't know what you're talking about,' she said with a disappointed little shake of her head. 'I only just met the man last night. How could you be so crass?'

'So I am crass, as well as a liar?'

The fury crossing his tanned, extraordinarily handsome features did not mar them for a moment—even though the sight of that fury made Ianthe's heart sink to her shoes like the heaviest boulder. There seemed to be no trust between them at all. But then, just because they had connected so perfectly sexually, it didn't naturally follow that everything else would work like clockwork, did it? Perhaps Ianthe had just been hoping for too much.

'I'd rather not continue this discussion in public,' she told him, her face burning scarlet beneath the scrutiny of the people around them, who were stopping in the middle of the street to stare. 'If you want to talk to me, we'll do it like civilised human beings in private— not with you yelling at me in the street! Give me half an hour or so, then you can stop by the hotel. I'll be waiting for you.'

'I will *not* wait for half an hour! What do you need the time for—to concoct a pack of lies to persuade me that you are not contemplating an affair with my father's friend? I have been deceived by an expert, Ianthe, and I am wise to the trickery of women. No, you will come with me now, back to my house, and we will talk there. Now!'

'No, Lysander. I'm not going anywhere with you!'

She naturally baulked at his angry, dictatorial command, but even as her lips lodged her protest Ianthe was mentally latching onto the words he had just uttered— specifically, the part about being deceived by an expert. Was he talking about his wife? Trying to see beyond the rage that made his fascinating blue eyes so stormy now, Ianthe knew she would not be able to deal with what Takis had told her with any clarity if she did not deal with this confrontation with a furious Lysander first.

He was reiterating his angry command, his voice rising.

'All right!' She glanced around her, saw the interested bystanders waiting to see how the show would develop, and sighed. 'I'll come with you.'

Without an answer, and not even waiting to see if she intended to comply, as she had stated, Lysander irritably rearranged his knapsack more securely onto his shoulder and, deliberately quickening his pace, headed back the way he had come.

Moving out onto the gravelled terrace that led onto the slender wooden jetty, its once-dark wood weather-stained and cracked with age, Lysander left Ianthe to follow him at her leisure. He needed some time to try and calm the barrage of disappointed and suspicious thoughts that were crashing through his head. Silently he acknowledged that the only reason he had demanded she return with him to his house to give him an explanation was because he could not help desiring the woman beyond reason. If he were totally in his right mind, not under some kind of carnal spell, Lysander would have told her to go to hell with Takis Koumanidis and never darken his door again. Beautiful, deceitful women were clearly his weakness, and he despised that weakness with a vengeance—because it was destined to bring him nothing but heartbreak.

Her footfall against the gravel, along with her soft, slightly weary sigh, momentarily made him forget his anger and turn around to survey her. One slim strap of her fetching pink cotton dress had slipped down over her shoulder. She made no attempt to rearrange it. Although a big part of Lysander longed to help her part company with the damned dress completely, he held onto his rage like a battle-scarred iron shield against her provocative enchantment, and did not allow himself to soften towards her to even the smallest degree.

'So, now you will tell me what you were doing in the café with that man,' he snapped out, his voice brittle.

'It was completely innocent.' Ianthe glanced distractedly out at the choppy, restless ocean—today the colour of kerbstone grey instead of vibrant aquamarine.

Her gaze was entrapped for a long moment, and Lysander was actually jealous that it clearly commanded her attention more than *he* did.

'We were simply having a chat, that's all.'

'A chat?' Lysander's lips twisted scathingly. 'He came all the way from Athens simply to have a *chat* with you? About what, exactly?'

She twisted her hands together and did not seem to want to look at him at all. 'I'm not—I can't tell you that. It's not anything like you might be imagining, Lysander, I promise you.'

'Why should I believe you? Do you not think that from where I am standing it looks highly suspicious? A man you only just met the night before at my parents' house invites you out for coffee the next morning, with no ulterior motive? I am not some uneducated simpleton, Ianthe. You are making a dangerous mistake if you think I am!'

He took a step towards her and she automatically moved back a little, her glance wary. Lysander immediately regretted his impulsive action earlier, when he had grabbed her in the street. It was not often that he let his frustration spill out of control like that, and he would be diligent not to let it happen again.

'Now, stop being evasive and tell me the truth,' he said commandingly.

Ianthe's head hurt with the effort of trying to rise above the torrent of emotion that was making it difficult to think. 'Who are you to demand the truth?' she spat out, her brow furrowing deeply in distress. 'When you've deliberately hidden the truth from me about what you do and who you are!'

'We are back to that again, are we?'

Clearly it was a ploy of hers, to distract him from his queries about what she'd been doing with Takis. Lysander rubbed his hand across his tense ribcage and subjected her to the full blistering impact of his hard, unforgiving stare.

'I had my reasons for not revealing completely what I did or who my family were. I did not set out deliberately to deceive you. I *demand* to know what you were doing with Takis Koumanidis! If you do not tell me the truth, then you will leave me with no alternative but to imagine the very worst you are capable of. And don't delude yourself that I will be easy to fool, or that I will forgive. I experienced my fill of your sex's treachery when my wife betrayed me with another man. I will not tolerate it from you!'

So it *was* his wife who had deceived him. No wonder

he'd jumped to the worst conclusion when he'd seen Ianthe with Takis Koumanidis.

For a moment all her naturally tender instincts towards him made her wish she could dispel the cloud of suspicion that was clearly tormenting him, even urged her to forgive him for lying to her. But she couldn't tell him what Takis wanted to speak to her about—how could she? She'd scarcely had time to absorb his astonishing story herself, let alone consider what the implications would be if it did turn out that she was the daughter of such a man! And, as well as that dilemma, he had asked her not to divulge the content of what they had spoken about to anyone, and Ianthe had felt compelled to promise that she wouldn't. No doubt the man did not want to sully his reputation amongst his family and friends, and it wasn't up to her to carry tales of long-ago love affairs that had ended in tragedy and heartache.

She couldn't divulge what they'd spoken of—but Lysander wouldn't believe her unless she did.

There was no choice. Hard as it was going to be, she would just have to tell the truth without revealing Takis's secret, and if Lysander's opinion of her was really so low that he could believe she was unprincipled and promiscuous, she would have to live with his horrible suspicions and leave it at that. No matter how much it might make her heart bleed.

'I am not deceiving you with your father's friend, Lysander. I swear it. I'm sorry that you're determined to think the worst of me, and that I might never have an opportunity to change your mind—but I'm telling you the truth. As a matter of fact, after today I'll probably never even set eyes on the man again.'

He so longed to believe her. How could she be deceiving him, he asked himself, when her voice rang out so clear and true and her eyes pleaded so beguilingly for his understanding? But Lysander couldn't help wanting desperately to know *why* Takis should deliberately seek Ianthe out and meet up with her on the island. If she had nothing to hide, he concluded, then why wouldn't she tell him what it all meant, and end this ugly suspicion and mistrust between them?

'Lysander?'

She came and stood before him, a becoming flush on her pretty face that had Lysander helplessly reaching out against his own good judgement to stroke his knuckles gently down one cheek. His palm opened to cup her small flawless jaw as though it were as tender and fragile as a child's, and he captured her startled expectant gaze once more.

'You are so bewitching and lovely that I would hardly be surprised should Takis Koumanidis desire to have you in his bed.'

There was a slight husky catch in his voice. His vibrant, searching blue gaze did not trouble to hide the flare of scorching heat that suddenly lit it, and the fingers that possessed Ianthe's jaw tightened discernibly. He could not resist her and he knew that would likely be his downfall. Yet if he had to visit the same hell that he'd visited before with Marianna—this time he would take Ianthe with him...

Before he had another moment to drive himself insane with more jealous, scourging thought, Lysander slanted his mouth savagely across Ianthe's, urging the ripe, feminine curves that so afflicted him with unforgiving longing hard against his body—feeling the heat between them explode into an irresistible fever of desire as her small velvet tongue tangled hotly with his and her hands slid up to his shoulders and then around his neck.

Tearing his mouth from hers, Lysander searched to find an affirmation of their mutual intent in her sultry brown eyes. When he discovered the answer he so feverishly sought, he did no more than sweep her high into his arms and stalk into the shaded bedroom where they had contributed their own brand of heat to the already steamy temperatures outside just a couple of days ago.

Barely undressing, they fell together onto the unmade bed that Lysander had left in such a hurry earlier that morning, their limbs tangling in a maelstrom of hunger and need as they could no longer deny dancing to the primordial tune that was driving them.

Ianthe had never lost her inhibitions or her mind so completely. She wasn't merely shedding her clothes— she was shedding the rigid cloak of self-restraint that had stopped her from experiencing pleasure or even feeling that she deserved it so many times over the years. Now she was revealing a wild, untamed sensual siren with no such restraint when it came to making love with this man. Lysander had unleashed a sexy vixen that Ianthe hadn't even known existed. As she rolled willingly with him on the bed, not protesting when he peeled off her pink cotton panties, then allowed him to position her astride his lean, tight hips, all her previous concerns seemed to fade into a hazy nothing. Her parents' deception, Takis Koumanidis's amazing story about another woman named Ianthe, her impulsive decision to change her life for the better in some way—they all seemed as if they belonged to somebody else. Not Ianthe. Not this brazen firecracker who couldn't keep her hands off this young, hard-muscled Greek god who was taking her close to heaven with his heated passionate touch.

'Lysander... I don't want to play. I want to— I *need* you to—'

'You have not said the magic word, Ianthe. *Parakalo.* That is Greek for *please*,' he teased her, his blue eyes burning possessively as his warm hands slid further up her slender bared thighs.

'*Parakalo.*' Her dark eyes were ablaze with desire. 'Take me now! Please...!'

He did not allow her entreaties to fall upon deaf ears. Willingly unzipping his jeans, Lysander freed his already painfully hard erection and thrust urgently into her hot moist centre.

It wasn't just the room that spun like a carousel run amok…the world did too. The pleasure that near drowned him was blisteringly amazing, and fierce masculine pride consumed him with satisfaction at the sheer lustful joy of her unashamed enjoyment of their lovemaking. The straps of her dress had both come precociously adrift down over her bare shoulders, and her dark hair was a sexy cloud of sensual silk round her lovely face as she rode with him deeper and deeper. The sounds she made were the sexiest noises of pleasure that Lysander had ever been privileged to hear, and the wild, unfettered cry that escaped her lips as she suddenly and violently climaxed echoed round the small unpretentious room with unhindered joy.

Lysander was not slow in following her to nirvana—pumping his hard hips urgently against hers as he spilled his loving with furious possession deep inside her. As pleasure exploded all around him and seemed to ignite a flame in his very soul he brought her head down to his and kissed her deeply and more passionately than he'd ever kissed a woman before.

He'd been to heaven and back. And if she turned out to be a wicked little deceiver like his wife, now he was more than halfway to hell.

CHAPTER TEN

HE PUSHED aside the mound of crumpled sheet they'd both helped to tangle and got out of bed.

'I'm going to get us a drink,' he told her, glancing briefly over his shoulder.

His jeans rode low on his tantalising lean-hipped figure, and Ianthe's covetous eyes followed his naked back, where he had stripped off his shirt. A little flame of renewed longing was flaring inside her and she couldn't suppress it. His loving was addictive. Her body glowed and throbbed fiercely where he had pleasured her. It was hard to conceive of his wife betraying him. The woman couldn't have been in her right mind. If Lysander were Ianthe's—

She ruthlessly snapped off the thought, because it could surely only lead to pain. He *wasn't* hers, and in all likelihood never would be. If he fulfilled his parents' and Takis Koumanidis's hopes then in a few months' time—who knew—he would be married to the man-eating Electra: two fabulously rich Greek families adding to their already impressive affluent and powerful dynasties by marriage.

And what if Electra Koumanidis shockingly turned out to be Ianthe's half-sister? She would be forever tormented by the fact that the man she loved was married to her own blood relation.

The thought of either or both of those shocking possibilities was akin to opening up an already sustained jagged wound with a carving knife. Remembering the story that Takis had relayed to her, Ianthe stirred herself out of her stomach-churning reverie and, pushing up the straps of her dress, also left the bed. She reached for the scrap of pink cotton that had been discarded in the passionate throes of lovemaking, then waited until Lysander had wandered out into the other room before quickly pulling it on. Slipping her bare feet into her open-toed sandals, she followed him into the tiny kitchen, unable to tear her greedy, admiring gaze from his bare beautifully toned torso and his serious, preoccupied profile as he reached into the small fridge for a carton of juice.

'Can I—can I use your bathroom?' she asked him, self-consciously curling her hair round her ear as he turned to acknowledge her.

'Of course.'

He didn't smile. Ianthe guessed that in spite of their torrid lovemaking he still hadn't forgiven her for being seen with Takis and for not telling him the reason why.

She had no idea how she was going to convince him that she had been doing nothing underhand. It seemed that her own jealously guarded principles had backfired on her. She'd torn into Lysander for not telling her the whole truth about how he earned his living, letting her believe he was just a photographer, yet at the same time she had not come clean about her own life. She had revealed very little about herself, in fact. No wonder he was suspicious of her motives!

'When I come back, perhaps we could talk?' she suggested tentatively.

He poured some grape juice from the carton into two long glasses on the worktop before replying.

'If you are ready to tell me about you and Takis Koumanidis then, yes…we will talk.'

'And if…' Ianthe hardly dared ask the question. 'And if I'm not? Because I told you—I *can't.*'

Turning his weary, accusing gaze on her directly, Lysander lifted his impressive naked shoulders in a dismissive shrug. 'Then you and I have nothing further to talk about, Ianthe. It is as simple as that.'

She was shocked. Her insides went clammy with cold. 'Even—even though we've just made love?'

'If you have deceived me with my father's friend, if you are even *contemplating* deceiving me, then I am afraid our lovemaking is relegated to nothing but empty and meaningless sex that we succumbed to simply to fulfil a very base human need.'

His cruel words made her feel dirty…cheap…used. Refusing to give way to distress in front of him, Ianthe glanced unhappily away and headed straight for the bathroom to cry her frustrated tears in private.

They had made love without using protection.

All the way on his drive through the busy and noisy Athens town centre to Takis Koumanidis's mansion, with the air-conditioning inside the plush Mercedes keeping him blessedly cool when outside the temperature was well into the hundreds, Lysander's fevered brain kept returning to that one irrefutable fact.

Was Ianthe using the Pill? Was he worrying over nothing? Nothing but an earthquake or an act of God could have kept them apart yesterday morning, when the heat of temper had slid hotly into the brazen heat of passion, yet how could Lysander *not* feel regret that he had not acted with a little more self-control? Now he was possibly going to replicate the untenable situation he'd endured with Marianna. If Ianthe were to be pregnant with his child, yet with her affections leaning towards another man, Lysander didn't think he could bear it. Though he had so coldly allowed her to leave his house in distress yesterday, in fact it had been almost impossible to prevent himself from taking her in his arms.

He knew he had fallen for her hard. There wasn't even the smallest window of doubt in his mind. That was the reason that he had returned to Athens and gone to see his father, to get Takis's address. If the man had either honourable or dishonourable intentions towards Ianthe, Lysander wanted to know about it! He would not pursue a relationship with a woman who desired another man as well as him…no matter how much he had grown to care for her.

He was shown into a palatial drawing room by a man-servant. His temper was simmering as he came face to face with Takis once more.

The older man stood by the marble mantel, puffing on a fat Cuban cigar, and for a long moment Lysander was mentally and brutally assaulted by a vivid picture of the corpulent businessman in bed with Ianthe.

Impatiently he steered himself away from the distressing picture in his mind.

'It is fortunate you were able to see me at such short notice,' he said abruptly, ignoring the ready smile that had overtaken Takis's plump, overripe features.

'Not at all, my dear Lysander. This is a true honour you do me! To interrupt your vacation twice in one week for me is not something I take lightly. My pleasure was immense when your father rang to tell me you were coming. I am only sorry that my beautiful Electra is not here as well to greet you, but perhaps we can rectify that soon. We have much to talk about…yes?'

Yes—but not about business, or his possible wooing of Electra, Lysander thought impatiently. It was another woman entirely that he wanted to discuss. Tunnelling his fingers through his dark blond hair, he sighed, with little tolerance for polite small talk.

'I saw you yesterday on the island, Takis. Having coffee with a mutual friend.'

'Ianthe? Such a delightful young woman.' The cigar was surprisingly extinguished in a huge marble ashtray on the mantel, and Lysander did not think he imagined the brief flare of agitation in the other man's eyes.

'What is your interest in her, Takis? You can be frank with me.'

Crossing the thickly carpeted floor, Lysander moved to a nearby stately white couch and sat down, his expression deliberately calm.

'My interest in her?' Takis shrugged, the gold of his wedding band glinting vividly against his plump finger. Lysander sensed his discomfort intensifying. It added disquieting credence to his half-formed suspicion that the older man was trying to persuade Ianthe into an affair.

'You understand the question, don't you?' Loosening his tie a little, Lysander stared unflinchingly at Takis, giving him no quarter.

'It is a private matter between me and the young woman concerned.' Clearly taking umbrage, Takis crossed the room to lower himself into the opposing couch to Lysander's, his forehead glistening unmistakeably with sweat.

'A *private* matter?' Unable to keep the tight rein on his

temper that he'd intended, Lysander couldn't help raising his voice. 'When, as far as I am aware, the two of you only met the other night at my parents' house, what could you possibly have between you that is so private? Unless you are trying to cajole her into your bed!'

'You are forgetting your manners, Lysander!' Looking almost apoplectic, Takis furiously mopped his brow and pushed to his feet again—with his weight and size, no smooth manoeuvre. 'Your father would not be happy to hear how rudely you have spoken to me in my own home!'

Lysander too rose to his feet, his greater height undoubtedly giving him a physical and psychological advantage over the other man. 'Leave my father out of this! This is between you and me, and I demand to know the truth concerning this situation. I am not leaving this house until you tell me!'

'This is *my* house, Lysander Rosakis, and you do not walk into it and demand *anything*!'

Clearly angered by this unexpected turn of events, and doubtless having surmised that Lysander was visiting him for a very different reason—to court his daughter—Takis stared furiously at the younger man.

'You had better explain to me your *own* interest in this English girl. I wondered why you had been so bold as to bring her to dinner the other night. Leonidas believes you did it just to spite him, because we both had hopes that you and Electra might find some common ground and start seeing each other. But it has just struck me that your interest in Ianthe must be serious indeed if you take another day away from your vacation simply because you saw her having coffee on the island with me.'

Lysander really did not want to have to explain his feelings towards Ianthe to anyone. He had barely explained them to himself yet. Loosening his tie a little more, he reluctantly held the other man's undoubtedly curious gaze. 'It is enough that you should know that we are having a relationship,' he said tersely.

'So you are sleeping with her, I presume?' Nodding his head, Takis sighed, as though coming to a private conclusion. 'Yes, I see that you are. So that is why you show up here at my house, making your angry demands to know why I was meeting with her?'

'I want to know the truth,' Lysander replied, his glance wary, preparing himself to hear the worst.

'I cannot deny that your interest in this girl is disappointing, when your father and I had fostered such fond hopes that you and Electra might… Well, that is clearly not going to happen now, is it?' Takis sighed. 'What I am going to tell you now, Lysander, has to remain strictly confidential between us. Even your father does not know anything about what I am about to relate to you. Do I have your word that you will not betray that confidence?'

'You do.'

Walking across to the door, Takis made certain that

it was securely closed. As he returned to the marble mantel and lit another fat cigar before launching into what he was going to say, Lysander's heart began to pump with something close to dread inside his chest.

Ianthe had sat up practically the whole night thinking about Lysander, and about what Takis Koumanidis had told her. Now, seated in the pleasant little courtyard, having her breakfast, stirring honey into her thick Greek yoghurt and inhaling the lush citrus scent from the lemon tree beneath which she sat, at last she came to a decision about what she was going to do.

Takis's story was incredible, and too close to home to dismiss as just mere coincidence—despite Ianthe's mendacious comment that such astonishing coincidences happened all the time. But, as intriguing as the story might be in prompting further investigation, she had decided exactly what her follow-up action was going to be.

Nothing. She was going to let things lie.

Her heart was actually infused with unexpected peace as she reached her decision. And the fact that she felt like that confirmed to her that it was the absolutely right decision.

She'd come to Greece to find out who she was, and— surprisingly enough—she had done just that. She was Ianthe Dane, beloved only daughter of Julia and Maurice Dane. Why go searching for the love of an unknown family she might be connected to by blood when she already had it at home in abundance? Takis Koumanidis had a daughter he clearly adored. What good would it do him if he discovered that Ianthe really was the result of a youthful romance he had experienced so long ago? It could do nothing but stir up trouble for him with the family he had now, and even though Ianthe didn't know anything much about him, she was not so heartless that she would want to cause him distress.

It didn't matter that for a very short time her appearance had made him think she might be his daughter and he had wanted to find out. The reality of pursuing that possibility might cost him much more than he would care to pay—not financially, but emotionally. The man already lived with regret every day that his young love had disappeared, never to be seen again, and that must eat away at his very soul.

Her mind made up, Ianthe spooned some creamy yoghurt into her mouth and savoured it. But even as she swallowed she couldn't help but recall the distressing way she and Lysander had parted yesterday, his coldness towards her not relenting one iota after she refused to tell him what she and Takis had discussed.

It was ridiculous that he believed she would contemplate having an affair with Takis—even without knowing the possible truth about their relationship! Was the man so dense that he couldn't see that Ianthe adored him? She'd even been prepared to forgive him for lying to her, though it might mean he was not as trustworthy as she longed for him to be. He'd had his reasons, he'd told her, and she'd longed to hear them and exonerate him of all blame. Now she wondered if she would even get the chance. She couldn't divulge what Takis had told her, so unless Lysander relented and accepted that she wasn't hiding anything incriminating it was difficult to see how the two of them might move forward.

She thought about the distrust. The lies. Yet it was incredibly hard to resist the immense attraction that he had for her. Her love for him consumed her every waking moment, and she had never felt so truly and vividly alive than when the two of them were making love. Knowing Lysander Rosakis had changed her fundamentally. And now, how could she return home and accept second best?

'*Kalimera.*'

'*Kalimera.* You don't mind if I have a look around?'

Glancing into the large and lofty room that was currently empty, apart from the photographic displays on show, Ianthe smiled easily at the very agreeable man at the front desk whose own smile was as warm and genuine as his welcome.

'*Parakalo*—be my guest. You are on holiday from England?' he asked, making conversation.

'Yes.' She pursed her lips at the reminder that she would soon be going home again, and realised there was more than one good reason why she would miss this lovely island. Everywhere she went, the people couldn't do enough for her, it seemed. They were friendly and helpful, and she couldn't help making less than complimentary comparisons between their generous openness and the sometimes much more reserved responses from people back home. 'But I don't want to think about that right now.' She shrugged and smiled, and knew the man understood that she wasn't exactly looking forward to her holiday coming to an end.

'Then please feel free to browse. We are open until ten o'clock this evening, so you can spend the whole day here if you wish!'

He had no idea how easy that would be for her to do. Being here amongst Lysander's wonderful and riveting photographs would be the closest thing to being with the man himself.

Ianthe hadn't seen him for over two days now, and she had begun to believe that he intended never to see her again.

Feeling a stab of pain jolt through her heart, she turned away to head for the photograph that had captured her attention more than all the others—the one she had felt a special connection to the moment she'd seen it. Iphigenia. Time seemed to stand still as she studied the anguished yet fascinating face of the old woman. She heard voices from the back of the room but didn't pay them any attention.

'I went to your hotel, but they told me you had gone out. I suppose I should not be surprised to find you here.'

'Lysander!'

Her hungry gaze drank him in thirstily as he came up beside her. Although he looked wonderful, in a plain white shirt and jeans, she could hardly see past the blazing jewels of his incredible blue eyes.

'What have you been doing with yourself?' he asked her, the smallest hint of a smile toying with the edges of his lips.

Thinking of you...just thinking of you, she longed to admit, but his glance still contained a hint of wariness that stopped Ianthe from blurting out her true feelings.

The fragile skin beneath her dark eyes looked bruised this morning, Lysander realised with regret. If Ari hadn't been seated at his desk, if they had been alone, he would not have been able to stop himself drawing her into his arms. But it was just as well that his friend the owner of the gallery *was* present, because now Lysander had to play things very differently where Ianthe was concerned.

Takis had revealed a fascinating, almost unbelievable story. If what he surmised turned out to be true, then Ianthe was his father's friend's long-lost daughter, and the realisation must be occupying the majority of her thoughts to the exclusion of all else. No doubt that included himself, he thought unhappily. She would hardly be contemplating the renewal of their relationship when her whole life was probably being turned upside down by Takis's revelation.

That was why he had left her alone for two days. And, besides that, he had all but ordered her from his house after she had refused to tell him the reason why she and Takis had met. Now he *had* to agree to letting her have some space…maybe a lot of space. Maybe a 'several countries between them' amount of space. The thought twisted his gut like poison.

She raised her guarded dark gaze to his. 'I haven't been doing very much, really. Just taking in the scenery and doing a lot of thinking.'

'Would you like to go somewhere and have some coffee?' he asked her, glancing across his shoulder at a contemplative Ari, watching them both.

Ianthe's heart leapt at the olive branch he seemed to be handing her. At least he wasn't telling her coldly that he never wanted to see her again. Had he maybe had second thoughts about pressurising her into telling him why she and Takis had met?

'If you don't mind me coming back to the gallery afterwards, I'd like that. I want to take another look at the exhibition.'

Reminding himself of how they had first met, his joy at possibly discovering a kindred spirit, Lysander shrugged in agreement. 'I don't mind at all,' he said, accompanying her to the door.

As he paused by the front desk Ari reached out and firmly gripped his hand, communicating to him in Greek that he thought the English girl was very beautiful and what a lucky man he was. Lysander merely smiled at the compliment without speaking, and followed Ianthe out into the sunshine.

CHAPTER ELEVEN

'WHEN we first met you told me that you had a lot of thinking about life to do.'

Leaning forward, with his hands resting loosely on the table that was shaded by a huge green umbrella, Lysander grimaced a little as he spoke. She had already been troubled when she came to the island…now he wished he'd persisted in asking her why.

He saw her frown, and waited to see how she would respond to his deceptively casual statement. Her hands were folded in the lap of her simple white cotton dress and she seemed particularly pensive.

'Are you asking me why that was, Lysander?' she enquired perceptively.

There was a tangible sense of unease between them that he very much regretted. After their last parting, when she had been so distressed by his apparent hard-heartedness, she clearly had her guard well and truly up.

'Yes,' he replied. 'Maybe it will help me understand.'

'Understand what?'

'Why you really came here. Why did you pick this island, Ianthe?'

He had begun to wonder if she had some secret lead that she'd been following—if she knew she wasn't as English as she'd purported to be. Why else would she look so Greek, would Takis be almost convinced that she was the daughter of his long-lost love…another girl named Ianthe?

'And if I tell you the upset of two days ago will all be forgotten? Our lovemaking won't be reduced to "empty, meaningless sex", even though I haven't told you why Takis Koumanidis wanted to meet me?'

A hurt look flashed across her face and Lysander pulled his hands back from the table and sat up straight in his chair. Making love with Ianthe had not been meaningless—far from it. Being intimate with her had touched Lysander's emotions more deeply than he could ever have dreamed possible, as well as giving him unimaginable pleasure.

'I should not have pressurised you about that—but what was I supposed to conclude when I saw you both that morning? Put yourself in my shoes, Ianthe.'

'It's very sad that you have such a lack of trust. Maybe in your shoes I *would* have drawn the same wrong conclusion, but I like to think that I would have believed my lover's word. I told you that my meeting with Takis wasn't detrimental to you or our relationship.'

Her pointed mention of lack of trust caught him on the raw. One corner of his well-shaped mouth nudging ruefully into his cheek, he slowly shook his head. 'I went to see Takis—' he began to explain.

She looked shocked. 'You did?'

'I persuaded him to tell me why the two of you had met. He was reluctant, to say the least. The story he told me could not have surprised me more. Why would he think that you might be his daughter, Ianthe? Is that why you came here?'

He saw her swallow defensively, and for a moment thought she might not tell him what he wanted to know. But her fingers fluttered almost protectively to her throat and she took a deep breath.

'My best friend died not long before I decided to come away. Polly had had breast cancer, but she'd been in remission for six months and I believed she was getting better—that she'd get completely well again and the cancer would never come back.'

She took a moment to collect herself and Lysander felt his heart constrict at her clearly deep loss before she pressed on.

'Her family didn't tell me that the cancer had come back, that she was getting worse…Polly didn't want them to tell me. I don't know why, but they seemed to believe that I couldn't cope with the truth. They had some notion of protecting me from it, I suppose—which was ridiculous, under the circumstances. Because they didn't tell me how ill she was…I didn't even get the chance to say goodbye.'

Wiping her fingers beneath her eyes, Ianthe grimaced, clearly upset. Unsure of how to comfort her, Lysander hardly moved. Instead he let her go on when she was ready.

'The other reason I came to Greece—which was a biggie, too—was that I found out that I was adopted just after my friend died. You can imagine how I reeled with the shock of it. And those are the reasons I came here. There was no ulterior motive, or a big plan to come to this spot in particular. In fact, I picked this island totally at random from a map of Greece. And, in case you're wondering, there's no evidence to support the idea that I might be Takis Koumanidis's daughter. Just because he thinks I look like the woman he loved and my name is Ianthe too, it doesn't mean that I'm his child.'

'Tell me more about finding out that you were adopted,' Lysander urged quietly.

'What's to tell? I was devastated.' Her mouth twisted a little in anguish. 'I'm nearly thirty years old, and all this time I've been living under the false premise that I was my parents' natural child. Now I know I was found abandoned in a hospital laundry basket with a note to say that my name was Ianthe. The name had been written in Greek. I suppose I came here looking for some sense of belonging—for a place where I fitted more naturally, seeing as I didn't seem to fit where I came from any more. I had absolutely no idea that things would manifest with Takis the way they did. It was a bolt out of the blue when he came to see me and told me his story. When he asked me not to repeat it to anyone else, of course I agreed. It's all speculation and supposition anyway—and why would a man like him risk bringing up a sad event from his past—an event that he isn't too proud of—and leave himself open to a scandal? Especially when there is no evidence to support anything. That's why I couldn't tell you what we were talking about, Lysander. I gave him my word.'

Her own reservations aside, the thought bombarded Lysander anew that Ianthe—his *lover*—might be the natural child of his father's friend. The friend who, ironically, had hopes for Lysander's interest in his vain daughter!

'So…given that it is all speculation and supposition, as you say, I presume you will be making enquiries about this possible link between you and Takis?' he commented, tanned brow furrowing.

But surprisingly Ianthe was shaking her head. 'I won't be doing any such thing. Whether it might be true or not, I already have parents who love me, who have done everything to try and make me happy—even though they might have been misguided in not telling me the truth about my being adopted. I have realised that I fit where I am more than I believed I did. I don't need to claim somebody else as my father to fulfil that need to belong any more. I already belong.'

'Do you realise the chance you might be turning down, Ianthe?' He felt complete perplexity at her casual disregard of the even more startling possibilities should she turn out to be Takis Koumanidis's daughter. 'Takis Koumanidis is a very rich man. His personal fortune is vast. You don't plan to turn your back on such wealth as if it were nothing?'

Ianthe felt a quiver of pain ripple through her at the reminder that money was clearly immensely important to Lysander, as well as to the people he and his family associated with. It made her realise that their affair could never go anywhere after she left the island. The millionaires and billionaires of this world did not have long-term relationships with women like Ianthe. No, Lysander would more than likely end up marrying someone just like Electra Koumanidis…someone Greek *and* rich.

She picked up her glass of water and took a much-needed sip to ease the dryness inside her throat. 'I'm fortunate that I grew up with a fairly comfortable start in life, but I have never believed that money was everything. I certainly don't see it as a prerequisite for happiness. So why would I feel that I was turning down some fantastic chance in not pursuing a possible blood tie with someone like Takis Koumanidis?'

'If you have to ask me that then you are most definitely not like any other woman I have known,' Lysander told her soberly.

He'd seen the proud angle of her head as she'd posed her question and thought what a remarkable person she was. It made him recall that she'd once said to him that she was attracted to him for himself and not his bank balance. It made him feel he should scoop her up into his arms on the spot and ask her to marry him, because she was indeed a rare woman.

As exhilarating as the thought was, Lysander did not feel he could make such a momentous step. He wasn't ready—not when he still harboured massive resentment against his father for introducing him to a scheming temptress like Marianna. His marriage had scarred him for life when it came to women. He'd already more than proved that he wasn't able to trust Ianthe. Look what he had put her through because of it! And there were no guarantees that their relationship would last beyond the early craziness of the intense physical attraction they had for one another.

But just as he all but dismissed the idea of pursuing the chance of maybe experiencing something deeper with Ianthe, he remembered his concerns about the last time they had made love—when he had been driven so crazy with lust for her that he had omitted to use protection.

'There is something else we need to talk about. Last time we met…in the heat of the moment, we did not use protection when we made love.'

He just came right out and said it, and he could see that she flushed self-consciously at the frankness of his statement. Her forefinger began to trace one of the little green squares on the linen tablecloth over and over.

'I regret that, Ianthe. If a problem should manifest as a result, then I—'

'A *problem?* You mean a baby?'

'If that should arise, then I will—'

'Will what, Lysander?'

Her eyes were very bright and very moist as she lifted her head to stare at him accusingly. 'Send me back to England for an abortion? Just like my mother was packed off to do, never to be heard of again?'

He had been going to tell her that he would stand by her come what may—whatever her decision might be concerning the child. Even if she *did* want an abortion, even if her wanting such a thing would be emotionally and psychologically catastrophic for him. He had already lost a child—he could barely contemplate losing another.

'I would never do such a thing.'

His handsome face was stricken, and Ianthe almost regretted her impassioned outburst. But the emotion of the situation and the cumulative stress that she had endured in the past few months had taken their toll, and suddenly she could not halt the furious tirade that poured from her lips.

'Why should I believe you, Lysander? Answer me that! You've already lied to me once—why shouldn't you do it again? You come from the same cold, heart-less, shallow world as Takis Koumanidis, don't you? Women are clearly expendable to men like you! You put your ambitions before love every time! You're probably too wrapped up in making your millions to think about something so trivial as someone's hurt feelings!' She pushed to her feet as anguished tears filled her eyes. 'Well, no doubt to your immense relief, you won't have to worry about an annoying little thing like me falling pregnant. Because, lucky for you, I'm on the Pill!'

As she turned to hurry away Lysander rose to his feet and put out his hand to try and waylay her.

Realising immediately that he intended to try and stop her flight, Ianthe threw him a contemptuous glance as she backed tearfully away. 'Don't touch me! And don't lie to me ever again! I'm sick of people lying to me all the time—I'm *sick* of it! Do you hear me?'

He heard her. And for the first time he realised how concealing his true identity and the extent of his wealthy background had compounded her belief that the people around her never told her the truth. Because of his own inability to believe that women liked him for himself, he had made a grave mistake in not telling Ianthe who he was. Now she believed him to be nothing but a liar.

He let his hand fall impotently to his side, and a tense muscle flexed in the side of his cheek as regret and dismay poured with equal force through his heart.

'Why don't you sit down and we can talk?' he suggested, knowing as he spoke that it was futile. 'You are jumping to conclusions that simply are not true.'

'Go to hell!' she flung at him, confirming his thought, and he could do nothing but watch her storm away, feeling renewed rage at his father for helping to foster in him the deep mistrust and arrogance that precluded him from being totally honest with a woman. Was it that that had prevented him from even saying sorry that he'd hurt her…?

His parents were enjoying cocktails on the terrace with a small group of close friends when Lysander made his way out there to join them. Galatea, his mother, showed her pleasure at his appearance immediately, and rushed over to embrace him with her usual demonstrative affection.

As much as Lysander was pleased to be greeted so lovingly, he did not waste time in stating the reason for his unexpected visit. Flicking his gaze across to his father, who was engrossed in conversation with a man he did not recognise, Lysander briefly touched his mother's arm. 'I am sorry, but this is not a social visit. I need to speak with Leonidas.'

Knowing straight away that her handsome son's formal use of his father's name meant that there must be some disagreement or unpleasantness brewing between them, Galatea frowned and brushed a lock of hair from Lysander's forehead, just as she'd used to do when he was a child.

'Darling, he is talking important business with the

Greek ambassador to Iran. Of course, as you are head of Rosakis Shipping, he will want you to meet. Why don't you sit down and have a drink with us? You can talk to your father in private when everyone has left.'

'What I have to say to him cannot wait!'

Unable to conceal the tension that was straining every muscle in his body, Lysander ignored Galatea's further entreaty to wait until their guests had departed and made his way directly over to his father. Briefly inclining his head at the distinguished man he was with, Lysander did not waste time with prevarication.

'I want to talk with you.'

He saw the slight annoyed flush beneath his father's olive skin. 'Lysander! Is what you have to say so imperative that you forget your manners? You can see I am talking with a guest. In fact, let me introduce you both—'

But before Leonidas could continue with his intended introduction, Lysander shook his head emphatically. 'Unless you want to me to embarrass you even further in front of your distinguished guest, I suggest you come and talk with me right now.'

Leonidas's study, with its opulent furnishings and dark cherrywood walls, looked sombrely unwelcoming as Lysander followed his father's broad, stiffened back inside.

'There are some things you should know,' he began, feeling the familiar sensation of floodgates of rage starting to open inside him.

'What things?' Genuinely perplexed, Leonidas shook his great leonine head and frowned. 'Lately you have become so unpredictable and hot-headed. I do not understand what is going on with you, my son. Does this have anything to do with a young lady? How did it go when you went to see Takis the other day? I presume it was not just business that you discussed? Was the beautiful Electra there?'

His father's utterly insensitive reference to Electra Koumanidis finally tipped Lysander over the edge.

'I did *not* go to see your friend Takis because I'm interested in his daughter. God damn it! Once and for all, I am sick and tired of your interference in my life. Is it not enough that you have already seen me married to a scheming, licentious bitch who made my life a living hell? Okay, I admit that I was responsible. I let my ego be flattered by her attention. I was taken in by her beauty and the practised charm that she wielded better than any actress. I made a bad choice, and I accept the blame. But you *knew* her true character! You knew her family well, and you were totally aware that she was incapable of being either faithful or honest. Yet because you craved the kudos of being associated with the aristocracy, and because her family could trace their origins back to the Dark Ages, you pushed her my way time and time again! And now you are trying to do it all over again with Takis's daughter!'

Unable to stand still, Lysander shoved his hands into

his trouser pockets and stalked the room like a lion going stir crazy in his cage.

Leonidas stayed quiet for several long seconds. Then, wearily threading his fingers through his mane of silver hair, he regarded his son with sorrowful eyes. 'I did not mean to cause you so much pain, Lysander. I thought that if Marianna got to know you, grew to love you— as she assured me she did—that it would help make her more stable. Her father thought the same. "If anyone can tame her," he told me, "Lysander can." I know that I let my own ambition override my common sense. Your mother has told me so more than once.'

'And she is right.' Coming to a standstill in the middle of the room, the strain of emotion clearly bracketing his mouth and flattening his eyes, Lysander let loose an audible sigh. He was frankly stunned that his father was apologising at long last for what had transpired before, and admitting his part in it, but he was still wary of his future intentions. 'Do not interfere in either my private life or my working life again. Do I have your promise?'

Leonidas nodded slowly.

'And you can forget about any possible relationship between me and Electra Koumanidis. Is that clear? I am quite capable of choosing my own girlfriends, without any assistance from you. And when I marry again—'

A spark of hope briefly shone in Leonidas's chastised gaze at his words.

'When I marry again,' Lysander continued, his heart

racing slightly at his own words, 'it will be to a woman of my own choosing, who I love—and not for any strategic or advantageous reason to benefit either the business or the family. Do you understand me?'

'How can I make it right between us again?' Moving towards his son, Leonidas gestured hopefully with his hands. 'I know Rosakis Shipping is more than safe in your hands—your skill and your innate business sense has more than doubled our profits in the last five years. You are a man of many talents, my son. I suppose I should just go more gracefully into retirement and let you do what you do best. Would that please you?'

It was an unlooked-for olive branch. Lysander relented. 'It would.'

'Then let us shake hands on it.'

It took a couple of seconds for Lysander to agree to the contact. He had resented his father for so long, and it would take time for past hurts to heal completely. But after they shook hands Lysander moved to the door of the study and actually allowed his lips to edge upwards in a smile.

'Keep well, Father. No doubt I will see you again soon.'

He left too quickly to see the visible emotional shudder of Leonidas's broad shoulders.

CHAPTER TWELVE

'WHAT would you advise now, Polly?' Ianthe asked out loud as she despondently threw some clothes into the opened suitcase on the bed. 'I feel like I've burnt my bridges at both ends. Oh, Mum and Dad will forgive me, I know…but Lysander?'

Sliding her hand down over the white linen shirt she'd grabbed off a hanger in the wardrobe, she briefly held it to her middle and shut her eyes in anguish. Why *should* he forgive her? She'd seen the pain and regret on his face as clear as day when she'd lambasted him with her impassioned tirade, but there'd been no relenting, no soft places in her that day for him to fall upon. She'd just allowed herself to think the very worst of him, of how he'd react in the event of her becoming pregnant, and now, because another twenty-four hours had passed without hearing any word from him, she was leaving without even saying goodbye. Running away because she couldn't face being hurt again.

Was that why the people she loved hid the truth from her? Because they knew deep down she was a coward?

What had happened to the vow she'd made when she arrived here? When she'd promised she'd discover an adventurous spirit inside her even if it killed her? Well, she'd been adventurous enough to fall hard for a compelling, attractive stranger and look where it had got her. Now she had a new wound in her heart to deal with...the kind that would probably hurt for ever.

There was no point in hanging around like some desperate, lovesick fool, hoping that Lysander might want to heal the rift between them and pursue a long-term relationship with her. A rift that had come about because she'd made a sweeping assumption that had no basis in truth.

Ianthe had judged Lysander on the actions of another very different man a long time ago, and found him guilty. She'd identified too deeply with the sense of abandonment and heartbreak she imagined her mother must have felt at being sent to England to have an abortion when she was carrying the baby of her lover, and she'd convinced herself that Lysander would act in the same heartless way her father had done...whoever he might have been.

Now she told herself as she continued to pack that no doubt he would be glad to see the back of her— running away or not. What should have been just an uncomplicated holiday romance for him had turned into a hassle he would probably rather do without. Well, the least she could do under the circumstances was leave with dignity and not hassle him any more. Even if the thought of not seeing him ever again was like being sentenced to solitary confinement for life. Because how did you willingly leave a piece of your own soul behind—never to be acquainted with it again?

The temperatures that morning on the scenic Greek island were especially gruelling, and as Ianthe waited in line with her suitcase and holdall to board the ferry that had just docked, which would take her back to the port where she would board a bus to Athens airport, she momentarily removed the white straw hat she wore to wipe her palm wearily across her perspiring forehead. She was sweltering in this unforgiving heat. In fact, because she'd managed to get so little sleep last night, she felt almost faint...

She didn't notice as a man dressed casually in a T-shirt and jeans purposefully pushed his way through the gathering crowd of people waiting to board the ferry. Ianthe only registered the black dots appearing before her eyes. About a second or two after that she slid towards the ground in a helpless swoon, and only missed the added calamity of hitting her head on the baking hot concrete as someone caught her and she was cradled protectively against a warm, hard chest.

'Ianthe!'
    The urgent pronunciation of her name was quickly

followed by an equally urgent-sounding plea in Greek. As Ianthe groggily registered the unforgiving brilliance of the sun piercing her eyelids, she heard the voice—which she now joyfully recognised—appeal to the people around them for help.

'Does anybody have any water?'

Somebody handed him a small plastic bottle and Lysander lifted her fully into his arms and carried her across to one of the sidewalk tavernas. An elderly Greek man quickly pulled out a chair and watched gravely as he carefully sat her down in it. Then, as Ianthe lifted her hand to her head to try and orient herself, Lysander put the bottle of water to her lips and firmly instructed her to drink.

The sensation of sharply cold liquid sliding down her throat had the same startling yet delicious effect of rubbing ice onto a brow that had a fever. It helped Ianthe ground herself once more. Now, as her head began to clear a little, she focused intently on Lysander's vividly coloured eyes as he sank to his haunches in front of her, his expression so concerned that she could not stem the intoxicating tide of hope that swept through her heart.

'What are you doing here?'

He did not answer her question but instead studied her solemnly, almost as though not trusting her to stay conscious without his help.

'How are you feeling now?' he demanded, running his hands exploratively up and down her bare arms.

'What did you think you were doing, standing out there in this heat?'

'I was—I was waiting for the ferry.' Ianthe bit her lip, her actions barely making any sense to her at all at that moment. All she knew above anything else was that she loved this man with an overpowering soul-deep and physical ache that made her blood hurtle through her veins with the most savage joy.

'Why? Because you were going to go home to England without even saying goodbye to me?'

He pushed himself impatiently to his feet, causing her no end of alarm—but then he dragged out another chair from the table and positioned it opposite her, so that when he sat down again their knees were practically touching. Sighing, he reached for her hands and enfolded her smooth palms thoughtfully, quite gently, into his own.

'Do I mean so little to you, Ianthe? Has our time together meant nothing?'

'No! It's exactly the opposite!'

'Then why go? And without even telling me you had decided to leave!'

'Because…because I was so horrible to you last time we met that I thought you wouldn't want to see me again.'

Her lips worked hard to smile but ended up in an apologetic grimace. Lysander kept hold of her hands, rubbing the pad of his thumb gently across her knuckles as he stared down at them.

'And I was so good to you that I mistrusted you the first opportunity I got—isn't that right?' He cursed beneath his breath as he remembered grabbing her in the street to vent his temper after he'd seen her with Takis. He'd had some idea then of just how much this woman was beginning to mean to him, but instead of exploring it a little further he'd preferred to believe that she was going to betray him with another man, just as Marianna had done.

Only Ianthe wasn't anything like his wife had been. She had honesty and integrity and much more besides, and he would be a damn fool if he let her go.

Lifting his intense gaze to hers, he felt his throat convulse a little before he spoke. 'I would never ask you to have an abortion if you found yourself pregnant with my child.' He touched her cheek very gently—the sensation of gossamer floating in the breeze couldn't have been softer, Ianthe thought, her heart aching for him.

'I know you wouldn't.' Her shoulders lifted in a small shrug and she found the smile she'd been looking for, humour coming to her rescue instead of pain for once. 'Anyway, I really *am* on the Pill, so you—we—don't have to worry. I'm cautious by nature and I don't often leave much to chance. Well, I never used to anyway. But I'm—I'm working on changing that.'

'If you did discover that you were pregnant with my child, Ianthe…the truth is it would be cause for celebration, not dismay.'

Letting go of her hands, Lysander flattened his palms

against his jean-clad thighs as he allowed memories from his past to flood back—and this time he purposely did not allow himself to push them contemptuously away because he could not bear to deal with the pain they wrought.

'I told you that I was married and that my wife died?' He waited to see the acknowledgement in Ianthe's eyes before continuing. 'The marriage was not a happy one. Marianna—she… Unfortunately she found it hard to confine herself to just one man.' When he paused, Ianthe remembered him saying that he'd been deceived by an expert and now, finally, she was learning how. 'I knew that she had made a fool out of me, but I was complicit in my own downfall. I let her stunning good looks and her declarations of love deceive me. I had married this woman for better or for worse, which is no small thing. When she swore to me that she wanted another chance to make our marriage work I agreed, because she seemed so in earnest. Anyway, she became pregnant with my child. I knew we did not have the kind of relationship where we would grow old together, but I truly hoped that if we were unanimous in our efforts the baby would perhaps make a bridge between us. We might at least rescue *something* good from our disastrous union. Unfortunately—after our last holiday here together on the island…Marianna miscarried our son and lost her own life in the process.'

Ianthe sucked in a shocked breath. The flash of deep

and abiding hurt that registered in the vivid blue eyes she loved so well had elicited such a wave of passionate emotion inside her that she was almost light-headed again. This time it was her turn to comfort him. 'Oh, Lysander. I'm so sorry. What you must have gone through…'

She placed her hand on his knee, on the soft faded blue denim that fitted so snugly, and immediately registered the heat from his hard, masculine body. Guiltily she withdrew it again—because now she longed to comfort him in a way that she definitely couldn't do sitting out here in public. She'd called quite enough attention to herself for one day by passing out in the queue for the ferry!

Lysander too had registered the instant branding heat of their contact in a violent ripple of carnal awareness that hurtled like an arrow of flame straight to his loins. But—although he desperately craved to be alone with Ianthe—there were one or two other things that needed to be brought out into the open before he could succumb to that great need.

'I did not tell you everything about what I do when we first met because in my position I am naturally wary of women who display a personal interest, and I have already made one catastrophic mistake. Because of that, it is not so simple for me to trust a woman's motives when I meet her. My family's name is well known in these islands—and so, of course, is the fact that we are very wealthy.' He smiled, creating irresistible dimples

that made Ianthe feel as if wild acacia honey was
flowing through her veins instead of blood. 'It was
rather nice to pretend I was simply some unknown
photographer holidaying on the island…especially
when fate intervened and I met the most beautiful girl—
beautiful inside and out—that I have ever met.'

Her body pulsating with excitement and an efferves-
cent energy that made it hard to sit still, Ianthe stared
at Lysander with all the love she had in her shining
from her eyes.

'How did you know I would be here at the port?' she
asked him, glancing tentatively across at the line of
people who were now boarding the ferry. Some thoughtful passenger had put her baggage to one side, with her
straw hat on top, where she could see it in full view, she
saw gratefully.

Noticing what he immediately interpreted as an anxious glance towards the ferry, Lysander felt renewed
concern pumping through his heart. 'I went to your
hotel looking for you and they told me you had left. I
could not come yesterday because I had to go to Athens
on business.' Later he would explain the challenging relationship he had endured for years with his father, cul-
minating in his disastrous marriage to Marianna—but
not now. Now he had to convince Ianthe to stay, not
hurry home to England. 'It looks like I got here just in
time. Are you still intent on boarding that ferry, Ianthe?'

She tucked a silken swathe of soft dark hair behind

her ear, ignoring the way that it immediately and prettily resisted her confinement of it. Her hand moved restlessly down to the skirt of her dress and a thoughtful, almost rapt expression stole over her lovely face.

'I love this island,' she murmured softly. 'It's going to be hard for me to go home and leave it behind…to leave *you* behind, Lysander.'

'Then don't go. Stay with me a little while longer.'

'But—'

'I am not just talking about until your vacation is over. I am talking about much longer than that.'

'What exactly are you saying?' She glanced up at him in surprise as he rose to his feet and extended his hand to help her to hers.

'I am saying that I want you to stay in Greece and marry me.'

'*Marry* you?'

She looked stunned, but whether that meant she was pleased or regretful Lysander could not tell straight away.

'Is it so inconceivable an idea to you?'

His brow had furrowed. Ianthe was quick to reassure him. 'It's not inconceivable at all! I'm just—I'm just overwhelmed.'

'I realised on my urgent dash from your hotel here to the harbour, to stop you from boarding the ferry, that it is the only solution to my feelings for you that I can bear.'

He was impelling her towards him even as he spoke, but Ianthe put her hand against his chest to waylay him from his apparent destination as his lips started to descend temptingly towards hers.

'Lysander—you don't have to ask me to marry you to get me to stay. I'd stay anyway if you asked.'

That stopped him. He looked suddenly grave, his brilliant gaze practically devouring her. 'That is all I need to know. The truth is, I think you captured my heart from the moment I saw you admiring the photograph of Iphigenia at the gallery. There was such passion and fire in your eyes—how could I resist? So, you see, nothing else but making you my wife will do.'

He was almost frightened to feel so completely happy. Just when he had practically resigned himself to a lifetime of bachelorhood, because he could not stand the idea of being betrayed again, he had fallen in love with Ianthe. A woman who truly wanted him for himself and not simply because she was mesmerised by his wealth and status or wanted to advance her own ambitions; a woman who not only shared his interests and passions, but with whom who he could envision growing old. She would also, without a doubt, be the most incredible mother for their children!

Lysander had felt sick to his stomach when he had arrived at her hotel earlier, only to be told by the officious receptionist on the desk that Miss Dane had left to go back to England. Thank God he had caught her in time!

'All right, then.' Sighing against his chest, Ianthe breathed him in like pure sweet oxygen, so much elation hurtling at speed through her veins that she was almost dizzy again. Except *this* time she had no intention of fainting! She wanted to be one hundred per cent on her feet when she said the words that were practically bursting to come out. 'I'll marry you, Lysander. I'll marry you because if I don't I know I'm going to spend the rest of my life feeling utterly miserable! I'd feel like an essential part of me was missing.'

'Then we had better not delay the wedding so we can ensure that never happens,' he teased, tilting her face commandingly towards his.

Ianthe's smile left her lips as she stared up at the handsome and loving face that gazed back at her with such undisguised devotion. Touching her fingers to his fascinatingly firm jaw, she secretly thrilled in the knowledge that she was allowed such a liberty.

'I agree. But first I want to make it clear that I'll never cheat on you or knowingly hurt you. And I'd love you just as passionately with all my heart if you were a pauper without a penny to your name! Besides, I've got money of my own, too. Before I left I put my business up for sale and…well, it's not worth a fortune, exactly, but it will fetch a nice little nest-egg for the future. When I ring home I can find out if…' She paused and blinked up at him. 'Why are you looking at me like that?' she asked anxiously.

Rubbing the small furrow between his brows, Lysander grinned at her. 'I did not realise that you talked so much.'

A rosy hue swam into her cheeks and she stiffened a little in his arms, suddenly self-conscious. Stroking back her hair from her forehead, Lysander murmured a tender endearment into her ear. As her blush deepened, his grin became even wider.

'What does that mean in English?' she asked softly, loving the sound of his own language on his tongue and thinking how incredibly sexy it was.

'It means that if you stop talking for just a little while I will be able to kiss you…'

'I don't always talk this much,' she protested, but her legs trembled at the possessive, hungry glance Lysander was regarding her with. 'I only talk a lot when I'm really excited…and happy.' Her dark eyes settled with unashamed longing on his mouth.

'Ianthe?'

'Yes, Lysander?'

'It would be very good if you stopped talking right *now*.'

'Oh.'

Words were swept from her head like stray leaves in a fierce gust as his lips passionately claimed hers, in full view of the line of people boarding the ferry and the approving smiling patrons of the taverna. And when Lysander did eventually stop kissing her Ianthe wished fiercely that everyone in the world could know happiness as wonderful as she knew at that moment.

EPILOGUE

One year later…

ROLLING over to embrace his wife's warm, shapely body, Lysander stirred into immediate wakefulness when he realised that he was endeavouring to snuggle up to empty space. Bringing his silk-pyjama-clad legs to the thickly carpeted floor, he peered into the bassinet beside the huge sleigh-style bed and frowned. That too was empty.

Hastily pushing his feet into leather moccasins, he left the luxurious bedroom of the new yacht he had recently named after his wife and mounted the steps that led up to the main deck two at a time.

The sight that met his gaze when he reached it made him feel as if he'd stumbled upon the most awe-inspiring work of art in a gallery or museum—so exquisitely were his wife and child framed against the backdrop of a shimmering moonlit ocean. Ianthe was wearing a long white nightgown, her long hair left loose down her back, and cradling their baby tenderly in her arms. Together they looked positively angelic. His throat tightened with emotion.

Sensing that they were no longer alone, with just the moon and the ocean for company, Ianthe smiled lovingly at her handsome, tousle-haired husband. Bare-chested, and wearing only midnight-blue pyjama bottoms, he took her breath away.

'What are you doing out here?' he asked with concern, his voice a little husky from sleep as he joined her at the guardrail.

'I was showing Polly the stars,' she murmured, a secret thrill of joy racing through her as Lysander's arm slid possessively round her middle. 'Have you seen them? There must be millions...' Turning their gaze upwards, Ianthe's dark eyes were filled with wonder.

Reluctantly withdrawing his glance from his wife's exquisitely lovely moonlit face, Lysander obligingly looked up.

He spared the silvery sparkling blanket that filled the sky a moment, then dropped his glance to place a small but tender kiss on his wife's incredibly soft cheek. 'There are only two stars I am truly interested in right now, my love,' he told her, smiling.

'Lysander?' Ianthe turned to him as a fleeting rush of fear flashed helplessly through her. Her heartbeat accelerated a little as she glanced into his incredible blue eyes. 'Sometimes I'm just so happy that I get scared.

Like now, when the three of us are together like this, under such an amazing sky like tonight, all safe and well. I'm afraid that it won't last…that something will happen to spoil it all, to hurt us.'

Even before meeting her husband on the island—when she'd been driven by challenging circumstances to embark on a personal quest to change her life—Ianthe had been determined to change her overly cautious ways and surrender a little faith and trust to the powers-that-be, instead of trying endlessly to search for some guarantee of security.

Her determination had more than paid dividends, because she'd met the man of her dreams and yielded to her feelings for him instead of believing that their future together was impossible. Now, as a result of her faith, they had a beautiful baby daughter too, named after her dear and still sadly missed friend. Not only that, but Lysander had healed his rift with his father, and Ianthe had done the same with her parents. Along with Lysander's wonderful mother, Galatea, there couldn't be two more devoted sets of grandparents in the world to little Polly.

'Do not be afraid, Ianthe.' Cupping one side of her face, then glancing tenderly down at the sleeping infant in her arms, Lysander gave a smile that was certain as well as loving. 'Nothing bad is going to happen to any of us, because we deserve this happiness. We are adventurers, you and I. We have negotiated stormy seas and we have found our treasure. Don't you know that the universe positively smiles on adventurers like us?'

Put like that, how could Ianthe *not* believe it? Feeling peace settle upon her shoulders at last, she lifted her face to be kissed. When her devoted husband had happily obliged, they turned and walked slowly back downstairs to their bedroom.

Just minutes later Lysander had his beautiful wife back where he wanted her, in their bed, his loving arms around her as she nestled against him, and their baby girl safe in the land of dreams beside them.

Legally wed, but he's never said… "I love you."

They're

Wedlocked!

Where
marriages are
made in haste…
and love
comes later….

This December,

Emily Vaillon was driven to leave her husband a year
ago. She couldn't stay with a man who didn't love
her—especially when she was pregnant. Now Luc
is back, demanding to see his son….

THE FRENCHMAN'S CAPTIVE BRIDE

by Chantelle Shaw

#2594 On sale December.

Look out for more *Wedlocked!* marriage stories
coming in Harlequin Presents:

THE FORCED BRIDE by Sara Craven
#2597 Coming in January!

www.eHarlequin.com

Men who can't be tamed...or so they think!

For Jack Cassidy it took just one unexpected,
long, hot night to unleash the kind of passion
that Lisa had never experienced before.
But did it also leave her carrying Jack's baby?

PLEASURED IN
THE BILLIONAIRE'S BED
by Miranda Lee
#2588 On sale December.

Brought to you by your favorite Harlequin Presents authors!